... of short stories is more of what Walker does best: write intimately about women's secrets . . . Walker is very good at making the personal seem general and extracting the aspects of an experience that most people – especially women – will identify with . . . her writing is warm and embracing . . . she is especially good at evoking the feeling of growing older and wiser'

Daily Express

'Walker gives us a deeper insight into experiences of black women in the segregated American South of the Sixties . . . the story becomes a poignant lament for lost love'

Big Issue

'The writing will linger on in the heart and mind long after you have turned the last page' *Sunday Tribune*

'Walker's simple, poetic prose is also beautiful in its sincerity' *The Times*

'Brave, philosophic and insightful . . . Dealing with issues of sexual fluidity, gender politics and racial identity, this is powerful medicine' *Gay Times*

By the Light of My Father's Smile

'Alice Walker in this, the most beautiful, the most compassionate, the most sensuous of novels, has created a masterpiece. It is one of the most life-enhancing novels you could hope to read. Flawless'

Mary Louden, *The Times*

'An exuberant mixture ...
conviction'

'Blends the sexual an ...
women's identity'

Alice Walker won the Pulitzer Prize and the American Book Award for her novel *The Color Purple*. Her other bestselling novels include *By the Light of My Father's Smile*, *Possessing the Secret of Joy* and *The Temple of My Familiar*. She is also the author of several collections of short stories, essays and poetry, as well as children's books. Her books have been translated into more than two dozen languages. Born in Eatonton, Georgia, Alice Walker now lives in northern California.

BY ALICE WALKER

Fiction
The Third Life of Grange Copeland
Meridian
The Color Purple
Possessing the Secret of Joy
You Can't Keep a Good Woman Down
In Love and Trouble
The Temple of My Familiar
The Complete Stories
By the Light of My Father's Smile
The Way Forward Is with a Broken Heart
Now Is the Time to Open Your Heart
We Are the Ones We Have Been Waiting For

Non-Fiction
The Chicken Chronicles: A Memoir

Poetry
Horses Make a Landscape Look More Beautiful
Once
Good Night, Willie Lee, I'll See You in the Morning
Revolutionary Petunias and Other Poems
Her Blue Body Everything We Know
A Poem Travelled Down My Arm
Absolute Trust in the Goodness of the Earth

Essays
In Search of Our Mothers' Gardens
Living by the Word
Anything We Love Can Be Saved
Sent by Earth: A Message from the Grandmother Spirit
Warrior Marks (with *Pratibha Parmar*)
The Same River Twice: Honoring the Difficult

The Way Forward is with a Broken Heart

ALICE WALKER

PHOENIX

A PHOENIX PAPERBACK

First published in Great Britain in 2000
by The Women's Press
This paperback edition published in 2005
by Phoenix,
an imprint of Orion Books Ltd,
Orion House, 5 Upper St Martin's Lane,
London WC2H 9EA

An Hachette UK company

3 5 7 9 10 8 6 4

First published in the United States in 2000
by Random House, Inc.

A CIP catalogue record for this book
is available from the British Library.

ISBN 978-0-7538-1972-2

To the American race

I wrote the story myself. It's all about a girl who lost her reputation but never missed it.

—Mae West

Contents

Preface

Thirty years ago I met, loved, and married a man from a part of the country foreign to me. He was of a culture, as well, that was foreign to me. As for his race, because of racial segregation or American apartheid, that too was foreign to me. Humor and affection joined us, more than anything. And a bone-deep, instinctive belief that we owed it to our ancestors and ourselves to live exactly the life we found on our paths. Or the life that found us. It was a magical marriage. Completely unexpected and unforeseen. Or even imagined. Or, in the part of the country we chose to live, legal. And yet, ten years after we met, we parted, in exhaustion and despair.

This book opens with a story, merging fact with fiction, of my version of our life together, when we lived in the racially volatile and violent Deep South state of Mississippi. It continues with some of the stories that grew out of an era marked by deep sea-changes and transitions. Stories that are mostly fiction, but with a definite thread of having come out of a singular life. It is dedicated to all those who love, and who seek the path instinctively of that which leads us to love, requires us to become intimate with what is foreign, and helps us to grow.

Acknowledgements

I thank Wendy Weil and Kate Medina, and Liz Fogarty for their work and thoughtfulness in bringing these stories to the world.

I thank Mililani Trask for her caring.

I thank Martin Luther King, Jr., for his impersonal, unconditional love that made it possible for so many of us to unconditionally love ourselves. I also thank him for having the courage and the clarity of mind to know and to say: 'I'd rather be dead than live in fear.'

To My Young Husband

To My Young Husband

Memoir of a Marriage

Beloved,

A few days ago I went to see the little house on R. street where we were so happy. Before traveling back to Mississippi I had not thought much about it. It seemed so far away, almost in another dimension. Whenever I did remember the house it was vibrant, filled with warmth and light, even though, as you know, a lot of my time there was served in rage, in anger, in hopelessness and despair. Days when the white white walls, cool against the brutal summer heat, were more bars than walls.

*

You do not talk to me now, a fate I could not have imagined twenty years ago. It is true we say the usual greetings, when we have to, over the phone: How are you? Have you heard from Our Child? But beyond that, really nothing. Nothing of the secrets, memories, good and bad, that we shared. Nothing of the laughter that used to creep up on us as we ate together late at night at the kitchen table—perhaps after one of your poker games—and then wash over us in a cackling wave. You were always helpless before anything that struck you as funny, and I reveled in the ease with which, urging each other on, sometimes in our own voices, more often in a welter of black and white Southern and Brooklyn and Yiddish accents—which always felt as if our grandparents were joking with each other—we'd crumple over our plates laughing, as tears came to our eyes. After tallying up your winnings—you usually did win—and taking a shower—as I chatted with you through the glass —you'd crawl wearily into bed. We'd roll toward each other's outstretched arms, still chuckling, and sleep the sleep of the deeply amused.

I went back with the woman I love now. She had never been South, never been to Mississippi, though her grandparents are buried in one of the towns you used to sue racists in. We took the Natchez Trace from Memphis, stopping several times at points of interest along the way. Halfway to Jackson we stopped at what appeared to be a large vacant house, with a dogtrot that intrigued us from the road. But when we walked inside two women were quietly quilting. One of them was bent over a large wooden frame that covered most of the floor, like the one my mother used to have; the other sat in a rocking chair stitching together one of the most beautiful crazy quilts I've ever seen. It reminded me of the quilt I made while we were married, the one made of scraps from my African dresses. The huge dresses, kaftans really, that I sewed myself and wore when I was pregnant with Our Child.

The house on R. street looked so small I did not recognize it at first. It was nearly dark by the time we found it, and sitting in a curve as it does it always seemed to be seeking anonymity. The tree we planted when Our Child was born and which I expected to tower over me, as Our Child now does, is not there; one reason I did not recognize the house. When I couldn't decide whether the house I was staring at was the one we used to laugh so much in, I went next door and asked for the Belts. Mrs. Belt (did I ever know her name and call her by it? Was it perhaps Mildred?) opened the door. She recognized me immediately. I told her I was looking for our house. She said: That's it. She was surrounded by grandchildren. The little girl we knew, riding her tricycle about the yard, has made her a grandmother many times over. Her hair is pressed and waved, and is completely gray. She has aged. Though I know I have also, this shocks me. Mr. Belt soon comes to the door. He is graying as well, and has shaved his head. He is stocky and assertive. Self-satisfied. He insists on hugging me, which, because we've never hugged before, feels strange. He offers to walk me next door, and does.

Its gate is the only thing left of the wooden fence we put up. The sweet gum tree that dominated the backyard and turned to red and gold in autumn is dying. It is little more than a trunk. The yard itself, which I've thought of all these years as big, is tiny. I remember our dogs: Myshkin, the fickle beloved, stolen, leaving us to search and search and weep and weep; and Andrew, the German shepherd with the soulful eyes and tender heart, whose big teeth frightened me after Our Child was born.

The carport is miniscule. I wonder if you remember the steaks we used to grill there in summer, because the house was too hot for cooking, and the chilled Lambrusco we bought by the case to drink each night with dinner.

The woman who lives there now, whose first act on buying the house was to rip out my writing desk, either isn't home or refuses to open the door. Not the same door we had, with its three panes at the top covered with plastic 'stained glass.' No, an even tackier, more flimsy door, with the number 1443 affixed to its bottom in black vinyl and gold adhesive.

I am disappointed because I do want to see inside, and I want my lover to see it too. I want to show her the living room, where our red couches sat. The moon lamp. The low table made from a wooden door on which I kept flowers, leaves, Georgia field straw, in a gray crockery vase. The walls on which hung our Levy's bread poster: The little black boy and 'You Don't Have to Be Jewish to Love Levy's.' The white-and-black SNCC (Student Non-violent Coordinating Committee) poster of the large woman holding the small child, and the red-and-white one with the old man holding the hand of a small girl that helped me write about the bond between grandfather and granddaughter that is at the heart of my first novel. There by the kitchen door was the very funny Ernst lithograph, a somber Charles White drawing across from it.

In Tupelo where I lectured I saw an old friend who remembered the house better than I did. She remembered the smallness of the kitchen (which I'd never thought of as small) and how the round 'captain's table' we bought was wedged in a corner. She recalled the polished brown wood. Even the daisy-dotted placemats. The big yellow, brown-eyed daisy stuck to the brown refrigerator door.

I wanted to see the nondescript bathroom. If I looked into the mirror would I see the serious face I had then? The deeply sun-browned skin? The bushy hair? The grief that steadily undermined the gains in levity, after each of the assassinations of little known and unsung heroes; after the assassination of Dr. King?

I wanted to see Our Child's room. From the porch I could see her yellow shutters, unchanged since we left. Yellow, to let her know right away that life can be cheerful and bright. I wanted to see our room. Its giant bed occupying most of the floor, in frank admission that bed was important to us and that whenever possible, especially after air-conditioning, that is where we stayed. Not making love only, but making a universe. Sleeping, eating, reading and writing books, listening to music, cuddling, talking on the phone, watching Mary Tyler Moore, playing with Our Child. Our rifle a silent sentry in the corner.

The old friend whom I saw in Tupelo still lives in Jackson. When we met two decades ago she had just come home from a college in the North where she taught literature. She'd decided to come back to Jackson, now that opportunities were opening up, thanks to you and so many others who gave some of their lives and sometimes all of their life, for this to happen. She hoped to marry her childhood sweetheart, raise a family, study law. Now she tells me she hates law. That it stifles her creativity and cuts her off from community and the life of the young. I tell her what I have recently heard of you. That, according to Our Child, you are now writing plays, and that this makes you happy. That you left civil rights law, at which you were brilliant, and are now quite successful in the corporate world. Though the writing of the plays makes me wonder if perhaps you too have found something missing in your chosen profession?

She remembers us, she says, as two of the happiest, most in love people she'd ever seen. It didn't seem possible that we would ever part.

It is only days later, when I am back in California, that I realize she herself played a role in our drifting apart. This summer she has promised to come visit me, up in the country in Mendocino—where everyone my age has a secret, sorrowful past of loving and suffering during the Sixties time of war—and I will tell her what it was.

Maybe you remember her? Her name is F. It was she who placed a certain novel by a forgotten black woman novelist into my hands. I fell in love with both the novel and the novelist, who had died in obscurity while I was still reading the long-dead white writers, mostly male, pushed on everyone entering junior high. F.'s gift changed my life. I became obsessed, crazed with devotion. Passionate. All of this, especially the passion and devotion, I wanted to share with you.

You and I had always shared literature. Do you remember how, on our very first night alone together, in a motel room in Greenwood, Mississippi, we read the Bible to each other? And how we felt a special affinity with the poet who wrote 'The Song of Solomon'? We'd barely met, and shared the room more out of fear than desire. It was a motel and an area that had not been 'cleared.' Desegregated. We'd been spotted by hostile whites earlier in the day in the dining room. The next day, after our sleepless night, they would attempt to chase us out of town, perhaps run us off the road, but local black men courageously intervened.

Over the years we shared Shakespeare, Dostoyevsky, Tolstoi. Orwell. Langston Hughes. Sean O'Faolain. Ellison. But you would not read the thin paperback novel by this black woman I loved. It was as if you drew a line, in this curious territory. I will love you completely, you seemed to say, except for this. But sharing this book with you seemed everything.

I wonder if you've read it, even now.

Our Child was conceived. Grew up. Went to a large Eastern university. Read the book. She found it there on the required reading list, where I and others labored for a decade to make sure it would be. She tells me now she read it before she even left home, when she was in her early teens. She says I presented it to her with a quiet intensity, and with a special look in my eyes. She says we used to read passages from it while we cooked dinner for each other, and that she used to join me as I laughed and sometimes cried.

What can one say at this late date, my young husband? Except what was surely surmised at the beginning of time. Life is a mystery. Also, love does not accept barriers of any kind. Not even that of Time itself. So that in the small house that seemed so large during the years of happiness we gave each other, I remain

Yours,
Tatala

Begging
Did I ever tell you about the woman who used to come begging at our door? I wonder if you met her? She was thin, somber, brown. Neatly dressed. About thirty-five, I would guess. Her head was always covered, and now when I think of her I feel there was something ascetic, religious, about her. She would suddenly appear, every three weeks or so, and she would ask if I had 'a few pennies' to spare. I always gave her more, of course. But she would not accept dollars, only pennies and, reluctantly, it seemed, 'silver money.' Each time she came I invited her in; she never accepted. You remember how hot it was in summer: I would offer her a glass of water; she always refused. I never saw her coming. I watched from the window as she left. I think she stopped at the Belts' next door, but I am not sure.

Who was she? She was the only beggar I ever encountered in Mississippi, where family kinship networks were so strong. Over the years this woman's unrelenting begging, but with such stoic restraint! has plagued me with questions. For I realize now that each time I opened the door, smiled at her and attempted to make her welcome, while I searched the house for coins, she regarded me with a coolness that I can only admit now was really hostility. Why? Also, no matter how hot the day, this neatly dressed beggar was never sweaty when she appeared at the door. Did she park an air-conditioned car just out of sight of our house? Was she, in fact, an agent of some sort, sent to keep an eye on us?

I could not bear to think of this then. I was home alone most of the time. Then, after the birth of Our Child, I was home with a small child. But now I realize, especially after visiting our old house, how odd it was to have a regular, well-dressed beggar appear at the door, obviously not that interested in money, and resentful of my kindness. I wonder now if seeing her there on my porch, begging—she held out one hand limply, carelessly, as she looked her hostile look—aroused my guilt at having a house, a husband who loved me, a child. Or was I always afraid that she was really me, or as I might become someday, out on the street, begging, with nothing but my—hopefully—clean rags of clothes.

This was at the same time that I was discovering the ancestors who'd died unsung and impoverished. I was uniquely placed to see how far the end could be from beginning and even middle. The writer I cared so much about, for instance, had died really poor. And yet, now that I am older, less easily frightened by images of poverty, now that I know poverty can also contain richness—deep friendship, for instance, or a faithful, devoted love—I wonder more than ever about the inner life of those who have been up and now are down. There is always the outsider's look at an impoverished life: it seems pitiful, a waste, a shame. Yet seen from within the poverty, perhaps a different reality might be sketched. A reality of lessons learned the hard, hard way that lessons *are* learned. Perhaps to finally know one or two true things about life makes up for the lumpy bed and chilly solitude.

And so I wonder now, if I asked you, if you would remember this woman? If, on my journeys away from home, she rang our bell and you answered the door? And what your take on her situation was. Did she accept only pennies and 'silver money' from you? Did she refuse dollars? Refuse water. Refuse to temper her hostility.

Sometimes, in my wooden house in Mendocino, with its yellow pine, barnlike slanted roof, I think of her dignity, if she *was* a beggar. I think of her going from brick house to brick house, in our suburban neighborhood. Behind each door a striving black middle-class family. Men and women who would rarely own more than their own houses and cars in their lifetimes, and know this as success. Women who would feel fear, to think of this woman out on the street—a phenomenon associated entirely with big city or Northern living; men who would speculate, feel embarrassed, and surely—one or two of them—prurient. Was this why she never smiled?

Her look, her manner, everything said very clearly: I will never work again. I prefer to beg. If, in fact, she was a beggar, and not an agent sent by the Klan, the White Citizens Council or other white supremacy groups of Mississippi. I used to wonder who slipped the 'The Eyes of the Klan Are Upon You' cards in our mailbox, which was on the front porch. Could this have been her task? And if so, how had she been recruited? To whom was she, or her children—I always felt she had children—a hostage?

There is a bitterness that does not dissolve when I think of black women begging. I feel their rage, and it is mine too. I am here and you are there, we say to the well fed. Why are we both not on the side of plenty? That is what I want to know, as I look into the eyes of someone who has given everything, if only symbolically, and is left with nothing. And the black woman begging does not let me get away with giving more than is asked. Once, in New York City when it still shamed me deeply to see a black woman beg—

not that it still doesn't, but my emotions have been battered into a more bearable numbness—there was a woman on the corner who reminded me of the stiff-necked beggar who came to our door. She too asked for coins, for 'silver money' only. In my shame and do-goodyness I offered a twenty-dollar bill. She chased me down the block to give it back. Grim, unsoftening. In fact, clearly disgusted with me.

There has been no response to my letter, which Our Child dutifully delivered. And one is not required. You are someone else now; someone I do not know. It is as if the young man I knew is dead, and you have colonized his early life. I know you sometimes speak of that time in Mississippi among people who loved you, so far away from Brooklyn and the tiny, contentious house from which you fled; but you must realize that the person you speak of is not you. But perhaps this is too bitter. Perhaps it is better to speak of the sadness one feels as the result of directly experiencing any sort of waste, whether in material or human terms. I miss you. We were good people. And together we were good. Allies and friends. Too good to have those years stolen from us, even by our grief.

Finding Langston
How were we to know Langston would die so shortly after we refused him a ride with us? I remember

introducing you to him as if he were my father. I was so proud. He was so seemingly at home in any world. The huge Central Park West apartment we were in, for instance, with its windows overlooking the Natural History Museum. How young we were! Sometimes, thinking of our youth, the image that sums it up is the back of your neck, just after you'd 'taken a haircut' and your brown shiny hair was shaved close to the back of your head and abruptly, bluntly, terminated, leaving your neck extremely vulnerable and pale. For some reason, I was moved by this; it always made me think of you as someone who would, and did indeed, stick his neck out. Langston liked you from the start.

I was too shy to notice anyone else, or even to hazard a thought about the politics of the gathering. Writers and poets and agents and editors, I know now. Some famous, some not. But what was fame to me? It seemed too far away even to contemplate. It was winter, I was, as always, longing for a father. How odd life is: Now, one of my brothers is very ill. He tells me, when I visit him in the hospital, that the father I always wanted was the one he actually had. He remembers my father organizing in our community to build the first consolidated school for blacks in the county, which was burned to the ground by whites. Then starting again, humbly, asking a local white man—who might indeed have been one of those who torched the first school—to let the community rent an old falling down shed of his, until a second school could be built. He tells me my father traveled to other counties looking for teachers, because our county was so poor and black people kept in such ignorance there were no teachers to be chosen among us. It was my father who found the woman who would become my first grade teacher. My brother's words are both fire and balm to my heart. Now, in my fifth decade, I know what it is to be deeply exhausted from the struggle to 'uplift' the race. To see the tender faces of our children turned stupid with disappointment and the ravages of poverty and disgrace. To think of the labor of Sisyphus to get his boulder to the top of the hill as the only fit symbol for our struggle. I am thankful that, when I went North to college, one of my teachers introduced me to the work of Camus. Sisyphus, he said, transcends the humiliation of his endless task because he just keeps pushing the boulder up the hill, knowing it will fall down again, but pushing it anyway, and forever.

We had the little red bug then, and you were teaching me to drive it, at two or three o'clock in the morning, when there was less traffic on the streets of New York. I loved those early morning hours: sometimes we would go swimming. We'd have the university's pool all to ourselves, in the middle of the night, and you taught me the breaststroke (so graceful!) and the sidestroke; and sometimes after swimming we'd go out in your car.

Langston left the gathering, of which he was star, and came down with us, and saw us head toward the bug. What he didn't know was that the backseat was filled with a large wicker basket we'd bought, our first piece of furniture, and a painting of turtles that proclaimed 'We are more alike than different.' Perhaps we should have thrown them out on the street, to make room for him. He was that precious, though we did not fully appreciate that then. He said, Are you going uptown? Hopefully. We said, with a regretful shrug, No, we are going downtown. We did not say there was no space for him. We watched, grimacing—for he had made us laugh, and more than that, feel comfortable—in the high-rise apartment filled with all white people, looking out over Central Park and the Museum of Natural History. He began walking toward the subway. And I shivered, for it suddenly seemed very cold. And he seemed the father I sort of knew. He'd given everything, been history, entertainment and example throughout the evening, telling wonderful stories of his adventures, as his eyes twinkled and the ashes from his cigarette—which rarely left his mouth— drifted down to dust his tie. Now he was tired and needing a ride, as my father might have, and I was going off into a life so different from his, I thought, that he could not even warn me about it, except cynically. As he, Langston, did later, after we were married, when he wrote to me and said: you married your subsidy.

It would be years before I learned of the elderly white woman who'd subsidized his early work, and what a 'primitive Negro' she tried to make of him, and of how he became sick from loving and wanting to please her, and needing to grow and be himself. When I read about this, how his health only returned after the last of the money she'd given him was gone, I wanted to return to that cold evening we had spent listening to his funny stories and drag him into a corner and force him to really talk to me.

Too late! Is anything more painful than realizing you did not know the right questions to ask at the only time on earth you would have the opportunity? There were other subsidizers in Langston's life. Mainly white men who supported and understood him. One of them built him a little cottage near his own house in California. Langston would live there peacefully for months on end. Did you remind Langston of these men? And did our relationship remind him of relationships he had known? And was he saying I did not love you? Or that love was only part of it?

We were invited to his funeral, and we went. We were husband and wife. It was a party. Like him, it turned us back on ourselves, while being superbly—with its lively music and energetic poetry reading—entertaining. At this 'celebration' and for years afterward I thought of his words, especially as you, unfailingly generous, supported me, supported my work. Read it, critiqued it, praised it, ran off multiple copies of it on the big Xerox machine in your law office. Sat in the audience wherever I read it with the biggest glow of all on your face. I had never experienced such faith before.

And now, thinking of the two of us sitting evening after evening reading Langston's stories and his autobiography to each other, as we mourned his passing and as Mississippi howled all around us, I hope this was the faith, the 'subsidy' of spirit and work, that Langston had also, in his own handsome youth.

Burned Bridges

Last night a friend and I were on our way to see a movie, in her small, far from new car. A helmeted policeman on a motorcycle pulled her over. 'What did I do?' she asked. He did not respond to her question: 'Is this your car?' he gruffly questioned her. She is a middle-aged black woman, portly, bespeckled and in dreadlocks. For fifteen minutes he grilled her about whose car she was driving and whether it was stolen. I sat in the car, leaning out the window. I had such a feeling of *déjà vu*. Should I get out of the car and stand beside her? Or should I remain in my seat? Even though this was San Francisco in the Nineties and not Greenwood, Mississippi, in the Sixties, I found myself suddenly grappling with a dilemma I thought we had put to rest twenty-five years ago. What is the proper behavior during confrontations with obviously disrespectful, hostile police? If I got out of the car and questioned what was happening and was ordered to get back inside, and refused, what were likely to be the consequences? How could they be dealt with non-violently, when he was the only one of us armed?

My friend's face was tense with suffering as she rummaged through a rather messy glove compartment for proof of ownership of her car. Having called in her information and verified ownership, he explained why he thought her vehicle might have been stolen: a sticker on her license plate seemed haphazardly placed.

Throughout their exchange the policeman, white, solidly built, with cold eyes and a graying mustache, showed no sign of human feeling.

'And why would I have stolen this battered little car,' my friend said, when we were finally free to go. 'And not a new BMW or a Mercedes Benz?'

*

On we went to see *The Bridges of Madison County*. A wonderful movie that reminded me of you, of us, the summer we met in Jackson, Mississippi. When I think of that summer I think of how perfectly my hair was straightened, and how neatly shaped. I think of the tiny, sexy dresses I wore. Dresses that bared my shoulders and rose above my knees. Dresses that said 'Africa' in a seductive whisper, not like the dresses I would later wear, that I made myself, from yards of vibrant fabric that made me feel like a member of a distant tribe. I shaved legs and underarms in those days, and was silky smooth all over. I had barely enough money to exist, but I did not care. Being in the South, in Mississippi, was what mattered. Not missing what was happening there. And almost immediately, we met.

It was like a dream, really. And also karmic. I was one of those who complained bitterly about white people having the nerve to be in 'our' movement. And yet of course I noticed you immediately, as a man. Your warm congenial manner in the café next to the law office on Farrish Street, as you shared lunch with your colleagues. Your laughter and flushed face above a crisp, cool blue shirt. Later you would tell me you noticed me too. I would have been in the company of Larry,* the lawyer for whom you worked, and whose errands you were

---

*Not his real name.

required to run. He had picked me up at the airport, and remained near, 'showing me around'. An arrogant, rich, Yalie in his thirties whose father owned a chain of hardware stores, Larry drove a blue Mercedes convertible as if he were lord of the world, and would later squire me about in it; as if this were something Mississippi saw every day: a handsome, suavely dressed, white man and a fashionably dressed young black woman who was actually perplexed to wind up, briefly, in his bed.

But there was no feeling, with Larry. Besides, he was engaged, I had thought, to the black woman who inspired me to come to Mississippi in the first place. Which made his seduction of me all the more puzzling. Not to mention my sleepwalker's response. I don't even remember having sex with him. I remember only a moment of standing next to a motel bed on which he lay waiting for me, and that I was wearing peach-colored bikini panties and a low-cut bra. He pretended an enthusiasm for what would come next that I felt sure he didn't feel. I did the same. I was embarrassed to be part of whatever game he was playing with the woman who loved him. And yet, in those days, sex was casual and often meaningless, simply because that's what it meant to be a person of those times. I understand now that it was she, so distant, cool, cut off from me as a woman, I was trying somehow to reach. Much later I would wonder if my behavior annoyed or hurt her. If so, she never let on, but continued her firm, unequivocal advocacy of the rights of black people and of children, and later married a good man and raised a family. It was she that I loved and admired, and wanted to be with. Not in a sexual way; at the time it was only men who set me sexually abuzz, but simply to talk, to ground, to move forward together as sisters. Because of my stupidity with this man who called you at odd hours to go to the cleaners and pick up his shirts, or to go to the corner and pick up cigarettes, I lost any chance of that possibility.

He was annoyed that you and I chose each other. Not because of anything he felt for me, but because you were an underling. A law student, yes, but also his servant, his gofer. Though you smiled, I could feel your humiliation, to be forced to do the trivial tasks Larry dreamed up for you: go to the pharmacy, the deli, the car wash. Make sure they don't scratch the paint or get grease on the leather top.

After weeping our way through the ending of *Madison County* my friend said: 'What this story proves is that love will find you.' And for us, that is what love did. And it had a sense of humor.

*

Because of the heat, ice cream was very big in Mississippi. We were always eating it. Do you remember? I came up the steep stairs to your air-conditioned offices—neatly renovated suites in an otherwise dilapidated building—wearing my littlest slipping and sliding dress, my slightest sandals, carrying a huge chocolate ice cream cone. You sat smiling at me from your desk beneath a window that framed your whole body in sunlight. Your hair was glowing. Your brown eyes filled with warmth. You loved, just loved chocolate, you said. Especially ice cream. I offered the cone to you, after taking a huge lick. You accepted it happily and licked rapturously, as if it were the best ice cream you'd ever had. It was a highly erotic moment, an eroticism heightened by the fact that just by licking the same ice cream cone a huge portion of the Old South that had kept my soul and my free expression of eroticism chained was forced to fall. That was it, for me. The moment we bonded, the moment we fell in love. I felt the wonder, the oddness, the rightness, the sureness of it. My body, without moving from my side of the desk, seemed to lean into yours. And yours, though you kept your seat, met mine.

Everyone could see what had happened. It was as if we'd fallen into a separate space that contained just the two of us, even when we were apart. Larry thought up more and more errands for you to run, even coming to your apartment in the evening to tell you what they were, as if he forgot he had a phone. I listened to him instruct you from behind the closed door of your bedroom, thinking of the journey we made together to arrive there. Of riding out to the Ross Barnett Reservoir with you and Carolyn,* the blonde secretary from your office, who clearly had designs on you, and who sat in the backseat with you and playfully put her foot in your lap. You and I were in one world, ours, she was in another. And when the police appeared, I was comforted to realize you and I remained in one world, the two of them in another. For of course the cop thought you and the white woman were a couple, albeit a couple of troublemakers from out of state. I was just a young colored girl tagging along. Carolyn played into this, snuggling up to you and trying to impress both the policeman and me that she was the queen of our car. But you had not touched her foot. And now you did not return her cooing attentions. Your whole soul was wrapped around my feelings, as I sat with the ice-cold dread Southern cops always inspired, telling me without words to have no fear.

And that is what you would tell me for years to come. That you were there, with me. That your chosen role in life was to love and to protect me. That I was safe. It was music I had never heard.

---

*Not her real name.

The other evening I got to meet the new civil rights lawyer everybody's been talking about. They don't talk about him just because he's a civil rights lawyer. They talk about him because he's got a black wife. And she's pregnant.

I think maybe I'm one of the first people to know this. They keep to themselves a lot, and you hardly ever see her. But I was in Estelle's Place; and way late, must have been around eleven o'clock, here comes this cute white guy, with brown curly hair and a cute, courteous smile. And went right to the counter like he was a regular, and he ordered chitlins. Yes, he did.

And you know how black people are. Estelle acted like it was the most natural thing in the world, but when she came back to the back where my cousin Josie is one of the cooks, they all just fell out laughing. She said: He's Jewish, you know. Like that explained everything. But it was funny enough to the rest of us without throwing that part in. I mean, how many white men do any of us see slamming into a chitlin joint in the middle of the night. He don't eat them himself, of course, said Estelle. But his wife's pregnant, and it's chitlins that she has a craving for. And she nearly split her sides, laughing.

I stood near the door, where there's a glass, and got a real good look at him. What struck me about him, to tell the truth, is that he looked happy. In fact, he was probably the happiest-looking person I've ever seen. You could just sort of feel it rolling off of him. And when he'd paid for the plate of chitlins, all nicely wrapped up and everything, he kind of waved at us back in the kitchen—where I didn't think he could even see us—and left. And we felt like maybe we wasn't such dogs, after all, for loving our collard greens, chitlins and hog maws, and our cole slaw and potato salad.

Passion

There is a languor I associate with being in love, and having satisfying sex. A dreamy look in the eye, a looseness in the joints. A dazed expression, even in the face of danger. And danger that summer was everywhere. Violence, everywhere. Pain and suffering, everywhere. Heroism too, everywhere. Knowing this, we stayed in bed a lot, doing our part to make it all real at the most basic level: making love to each other, we worshiped the miracle of what was possible.

The first time, though, was awkward. And why not? We made love in Carolyn's apartment, where I stayed, sleeping on a fold-up cot in her small living room. I think it was bad because she was in her room asleep. Or was she? It is hard now to imagine that we were so desperate that we might have done this. Invaded her space in this way. Our only excuse, perhaps, is that in such a violent, racially polarized city we had nowhere else to go. Going with you to your room so shortly after meeting would have felt brazen, presumptuous. You also had a room-mate. I was shocked by the intense heat of your body, by the profusion of hair on your chest, your wide shoulders and gentle hands. Even though the sex was off, our breathing together was not, and it was the perfect harmony of our breaths that I fell asleep, after you left, thinking about.

It wasn't long before we were trying to explain to each other what it was we did. You were taking depositions from dispossessed sharecroppers who'd opposed their bosses and been thrown off the land. I was doing freelance movement work, but really I was writing a novel that required a closer look at the South. You read the writing I had done so far, in a notebook I carried with me everywhere, and became my champion, instantly. Your work, defending and empowering black people who might have been my parents, my family, endeared you to me, effortlessly. We were a couple: black and white to the people who saw us pass by on the street, but already Sweetheart and Darling to ourselves.

It really did seem at times as if our love made us bulletproof, or perhaps invisible. When we walked down the street together the bullets that were the glances of the racist onlookers seemed turned back and sent hurtling off into outer space. The days passed in a blur of hard work, constant awareness of violence, and inutterable tenderness between ourselves. At the end of the long afternoons listening to the sorrows of your clients, we crept close to the cranky air conditioner in your room—just by the bed—and read poetry to each other. Yeats, Walt Whitman, cummings. We spent the humid evenings learning to give pleasure to each other. Soon, our shaky start in Carolyn's living room was forgotten. One day we made love during a rousing afternoon thunderstorm. Torrents of rain cascaded down the streets; the air was blue with it. Lightning streaked our bodies with silver. Nature supports what *is*, we felt, as our bodies moved passionately together. We were a part of it, no questions asked. When I left for New York, you promised to join me, later, at the end of summer. Your last year of law school was coming up; I was going back to the cheap, cockroach-infested apartment and typewriter-on-the-kitchen-table life of the beginning writer.

Handling It

I think I am handling it all very well. Preparing to see you again, to actually engage in meaningful talk, after so many years. Our Child has arranged for us to meet with her and her therapist in a brownstone in Upper Manhattan. Because it is the beginning of summer and already quite warm, I am wearing a long, thin cotton dress and a light jacket. Something about the dress feels strange, and I do not realize what it is until I get out of the taxi at the therapist's door. I have put it on backward. You have arrived early and are sitting in the therapist's reception room. We say hello, and embrace briefly. I duck into the toilet and swiftly rearrange my dress. When I come out you and Our Child and the therapist are seated, chatting.

For years Our Child has been the only visible, public evidence of our years together. She sits tall and poised. Twenty-five, and used to making her own way in the world. Her only obstacle, she feels, a certain ignorance about who her parents really are. I ask that the seating be rearranged so that you are seated between us. You are compliant, and as you move across me to take your seat I look at you. You are heavier, your hair is thinning. I sense both weariness and wariness. I believe this is the first time you've set foot in a psychiatrist's office. Your brown eyes smile, and I can now see that it is your eyes that smile in situations like this—that you feel threatened by but determined to endure—not you. I sense an unsmiling you carefully concealed behind your face. The same unsmiling you who smiled when the racists called you 'Jew lawyer', and reminded you they'd already lynched two 'outside agitator Jews from New York' shortly before you arrived to work in Mississippi. In your stylish, rumpled suit and sensible tie, you look like the successful corporate lawyer and devoted nuclear family head in Westchester County that you now are.

It is difficult to believe we were once married to each other. Or that when we were, you would occasionally play poker all night, sleep much of the day, and get to the office just as most offices were closing, at five o'clock. Or that, routinely, you would go to work around noon and stay at the office until late at night. Sometimes I would visit you there, and we'd have a picnic on your desk around midnight. And work together, snuggle and kiss well into morning. Like Our Child, who inherited this trait from you, so that getting her out of bed before noon is a chore, you are a night person. Or you were a night person. Apparently now you are not. You get up, according to Our Child, at the crack of dawn, catch a train, and come into Manhattan at an hour you and I would have been still cuddled up together in bed, oblivious of the time. I remember how shocked I was, when she told me this. You, shaved and dressed, on a moving train, headed for New York City, before ten in the morning? Maybe even before nine? My heart ached for you.

The therapist wants to know what it is we want from the two-hour session Our Child has arranged for. I wonder this myself. In my case, it is some kind of closure. My mind flashes on the last brief conversation we had after receiving verification of our divorce. We'd left the federal building in which severance had occurred—whether in Brooklyn or Manhattan, I no longer recalled—and stood, after ten years of marriage, suddenly free, legally, of each other. And because we were now legally free of each other, I was feeling very close. The humor with which I was able to see so much of our life together, suddenly returned. I smiled at you, gave a sigh of relief and said: 'Well, that's over. Let's go somewhere and have a cup of tea.' But your face reflected none of my lightheartedness. You were morose. 'No thank you,' you said. 'I have to get back to the office.' It was a response emblematic of our problem. My face fell. However, still determined to prove to myself at least that divorce need not mean the end of simple civility, I stuck out my hand. You reluctantly, it seemed to me, took it. We shook hands woodenly, like a couple of strangers, and you turned and disappeared down the street. And I must have said, to the emotions crowding around my chest: Get away from me.

Our Child is speaking. What she wants, she says, is to better understand something that has always puzzled her. She has been the go-between all these years. Eighteen, or so. What she has noticed about each of us when we speak of the other is a kind of wistfulness. We seem to her bemused, often. Puzzled, frequently. Not quite sure ourselves what happened to us. The moment she describes us in this way, I see that it is the truth, and I feel an enormous wave of pity for us, her parents. What did happen to us? It seems now a question well worth considering.

You are sitting, still smiling, your legs crossed. The therapist is looking from you to me. What did happen? she asks. You are silent, waiting, as if you'd also like to know. Two hours will go quickly, I know. I decide to take the plunge.

I tell her about our courtship and early marriage. The sense we both had of finding, and bonding with, a miraculously compatible mate. The long years of trying to accommodate ourselves to a violent, and often boring environment. The isolation. The racism. The sexism. The slow breakdown of my spirit after I'd finished this novel or that, this story or that, this poem or that, and looked about and found little to amuse, divert or sustain me. Of your retreat into the secluded quiet of your office, night after night. The loneliness. The old conflict resurfacing between loyalty to 'other' and loyalty to myself.

It was the same struggle I'd faced with my mother, I said. I always understood her work was important. She had to be away from home in order for there to *be* a home. It was her earnings that meant food, clothes, a toothbrush.

A roof over our heads. I dared not complain. And yet I missed her with every fiber of my being. I died each day she was away. Yet, I could say nothing. It was the same in my marriage. Each day my husband went out, often in danger, to slay the dragons of racism and ignorance that proliferated in Mississippi. Many, many people depended on him. More than I did, I sometimes thought. How could I say I also needed him?

The therapist is a middle-aged refugee from Latvia. She has a thoughtful face and a faint accent. The language of her body says: this is a space in which it is safe to express. Her large Irish wolfhound lies in front of the tiled fireplace, asleep. What a difference such a person, such an ear, would have made in our lives all those years ago, I think. And flash on the five-mile bike ride that had taken me for several weeks to the office of Dr. Hickerson, who casually prescribed Valium, and sent me numbly careening on my way. She did not care enough to suggest perhaps we were simply trying to do too much. That we were throwing our young lives against a system that had crushed lovers and idealists for centuries.

I sigh, into the quiet room. I think, I say, that Mississippi, living interracially, attempting to raise a child, attempting to have a normal life, wore us out. I think we were exhausted. In our tiredness we turned away from each other. Next to me on the couch, I feel you relax. Perhaps you anticipated blame.

But how can I blame you for being human? For wearing out. For running on empty eventually. Just as I did. Now you begin to talk. You mention how, in the final days in Mississippi, you became afraid to leave me alone in the house. That one day you locked the door behind you and I accused you of locking me in. That was the day, you say, you knew we had to leave. I don't remember this particular day, but I certainly do recall the feeling of being incarcerated. Solitary confinement might be ideal for certain forms of mental creativity, but it is horrible for someone who craves a social world, whose spirit yearns for the refreshment of companionship. Between 'projects,' my books, there were days that contained only a scream into the silence. I combated this by teaching at two of the local black colleges, for practically no money. I planted trees and flowers. I learned to shop in a way that took hours rather than minutes. I joined an exercise club, to which my slim, bored neighbor Phyllis, and I went each week. I quilted, I began making a rug. I actually did needlepoint. I talked to my mother on the phone.

Our Child does not remember any of the happiness that surrounded her arrival in our house. And yet, it is this happiness for which she yearns. It is the security of two doting parents, adoringly attentive, adoringly present, that is the quality of comfort she misses. She has become angry at us over the years because no matter what she has tried, this quality of being completely loved by both of us, together, has remained beyond her reach. I feel sad for her. I see the little girl running to the door at the sound of her father's car, a huge brown and black Toronado that was always, because of its incongruous stylishness, comical for a civil rights lawyer. I see her father fly out from around the car, running to meet her wet and openhearted kisses, her widespread, chubby arms. I see him down on one knee, lifting her against his chest, his wide face transparent with love. I see myself standing, smiling, in the doorway. In his eagerness to embrace and kiss me as well, his thin lips are already stuck out. He is the only white person in the neighborhood at this hour of the day, but even if I think of this it is with amusement. The three of us collide in the doorway, laughing to think we have outwitted racism and racist laws one more time and lived to love another day.

On such an upbeat day I would have worked well, whether at typewriter, quilting or flower planting. Our Child and I would have played. She would have napped. I would have shopped, driven out for a walk around the reservoir, taught. But most important, you would have come home in time for dinner, and would perhaps spend the evening at home, not, as was often the case, in the office, where one or another case of a black family being terrorized by whites would have called you, immediately after dinner, and compelled you to work on it through the night. .

I have a question to ask you. I look at the therapist to see if it is okay. She nods. Why do you work so much? You look surprised by the question. I don't know, you say. I've always done it. I know this is true. I remember how, when we met, you were still selling life insurance—a lucrative job finagled from a friend of the family, by your mother—which you'd done for years, even though you were a law student and so young. You also taught swimming at the law school and took care of the pool. In fact, you were poor. You owned two pairs of slacks, one blue and one yellow, and the shiny hazel-colored suit in which you were married. You owned two ties and half a dozen shirts. Two pairs of shoes. I too could pack everything I owned, including my typewriter, in a couple of suitcases. When we finally moved in together, in your room overlooking Washington Square Park, there was an absence of clutter simply because our possessions were so few. A bedspread doubled as a tablecloth, a folding table doubled as a desk. Your single bed seemed fine and comfortable for the two of us. We shared a bathroom with your suitemate.

*

I wanted to scream at you, as I'd wanted to scream at my mother: Come back! Don't go to work! I miss you! I am in danger while you are gone! But now it is too late to scream this, even though I finally understand this is exactly what I should have screamed. We were divorced seventeen years ago. I cannot stop the tears, however, and they roll down my cheeks, just as they did after you closed the door to our house, those lonely mornings so many years ago. I take tissues from the box at my left. Glancing down as I wipe my face, I see your well-shod foot. The cuffs of your designer slacks. We have both done phenomenally well, materially. It strikes me suddenly as astonishing. Because it was never something we set out to do. Today I own large, beautiful houses, over-compensation for the shacks in which I was raised; and when I travel, my hotel suite is nearly as large as our old house. You have a powerful New York law firm, and the best of whatever Westchester County has to offer. There is a rumor that you play golf. I confess that I can't quite imagine this. Both of us have been hard workers all our lives, and yet much of what we have today—at least speaking for myself—seems to have fallen into our laps. Or do all poor people who become successful in America feel like this?

What is this road on which there is so much beauty and so much pain? So much love and so much suffering? Such surprise. How can it be that we have lost each other all these years? That even though it took my mother thirteen years to die, you never sent her a card. It would have been easier for me to believe you murdered someone than that this could happen. Was it because, on meeting you, she hurt your feelings by identifying you with the only label her fundamentalist Christian upbringing gave her for Jews: Christ-killer. Or that she said, even though she knew better, because I had told her you were only twenty-two, that you seemed like an old man. Once again I look down at your stylish Italian leather shoes. Even your feet have changed, I think, recalling the black 'space' shoes you used to wear because your Pisces feet (fish feet) were so tender and often sore. You appeared to roll a bit as you walked, in an attempt to alleviate the discomfort; perhaps this is what struck her as odd, as old. An old man's walk. But it was like her, in any case, to be critical of whomever I brought home. Except for Porter, the young man I fell in love with when I was six and became intimate with when I was sixteen. This was her son-in-law, the one she chose, the one she wanted, though he and I separated as friends when I was eighteen. She never said about him, as she did about every other boy or man: he has a homely face, you will soon tire of it; his feet are slightly splayed, his wrists are too thin, he will be bald before he's thirty. I was dismayed, of course, that she could not really see you. That my father could not. My whole family could not. To them, you were for many years merely a white male blur wearing clothing. No matter how gentle you appeared, you struck an ancient terror in their hearts. To them, all white people had a vampire quality, they were seen as people who devour, who suck dry. They waited for this to happen to me. And there was the awful history of black women and white men.

Our Child is curious about her birth, though I have told her about it many times. She turns to you and says: I understand you were away somewhere when Mama went into labor. You tell her the story of being in court, when the word came. Of arguing a school desegregation case before the Fifth Circuit Court of Appeals in New Orleans. Of being told by one of the judges that having planted the seed, you didn't have to be present for the harvest. But that you hadn't listened, but hastened home, to accompany me to the hospital. And that, while I was still in the hospital, your mother also came, and set up camp in our house. At last accepting there was another woman in your life. But there was no one but you to visit me in the hospital or am I forgetting someone? Perhaps our friend Barbara, perhaps the secretaries from your office? In any case, I only remember you. Your pale, stricken face and fear at the sight of blood. Your apparent helplessness. My attention so focused on the pain that seemed about to drown me, that I could not offer anything except muffled silence. For my gynecologist I had chosen the only woman doctor—it was rumored she was lesbian—in the hospital. Her bedside manner turned out to be chilly and abrupt. She waited until the last possible moment to relieve me of pain—at the precise moment I felt the pain might be turning into its opposite, a completion for which my body has never ceased to yearn. Her hands had not an ounce of gentleness. Her episiotomy unnecessarily savage. No one could believe we were there together, married, to have our neither black nor white child. We were a major offense. And yet, the side of this experience that I have consciously remembered all these years is the look in Our Child's eyes when she emerged into our world: a long, searching look at you, then an equally inquiring glance at me. It shocked us; it felt so much like an old acquaintance re-entering a room we happened to be in. And I remember the red roses, dozens of them, behind which your beaming face, later in my room, appeared. The black nurses delighted in the discomfiture of the white ones, who could not, as the black ones could not, fathom such behavior. Most white fathers of black children in the South never even saw the mothers pregnant, not to mention actually saw the child after birth. The white nurses were soon captivated by your charm and good looks, casting you in the role of a contemporary Rhett Butler, but of course bemoaning the fact that you had chosen the wrong Scarlett. We were the nightmare their mothers had feared, the hidden delight generations of their fathers enjoyed. We were what they had been taught was an impossibility, as unlikely as a two-headed calf: a happy interracial couple, married (and they knew this was still illegal in their state), having a child, whom we obviously cherished, together.

Did you ever wonder how we must have appeared to our mothers? I have often wondered this. Once, in the days following the birth of Our Child—for she would not speak of sex or childbirth before I had a child—my mother broke a self-imposed taboo to speak to me of rape. Or rather, of how she had avoided rape. I have a feeling now that she was the kind of woman who would have said a woman could not be raped: though her own light-colored face belied this, surely. People who are routinely violated over centuries make curious denials. But I would speak to her of rape, as I spoke to her of everything that mattered. And she told me the following story: That one day she and her sisters and brothers were walking down a deserted road, and white men began to make advances toward and then to chase the girls. Her brothers ran away, leaving the girls to fight or run as best they could. She understood their behavior, of course, but there was sadness in her telling of it. If they had tried to protect their sisters they would have been murdered without a thought. Luckily, she and her sisters were strong and fast; they simply outran their would-be rapists.

Do you remember how I used to suddenly develop passions? I am still that way. In Mississippi I began to crave arrowheads. It came upon me as suddenly as the desire, years before, to write poetry. I hungered for the sight of them. I ached for the feel of them in my hand. Now I think this was perhaps another beginning of the endless understanding of who I really am. In childhood I must have longed for pebbles, for certain tree leaves, for the sight of the river. For the taste of earth. I remember that I placed an ad in the paper, and that there was a response. I began to collect arrowheads. A few wondrously whole, many broken or chipped. All precious to me. I even collected the stone from a tomahawk. I collected arrowheads for years, and then began the slow, deeply satisfying ritual of passing them on. And yet, since then I've never been without. On the kitchen table where I am writing this there is a small wooden bowl from Africa that holds a remnant of what was once a large collection. Our Child has never known her mother without arrowheads, without Native American jewelry, without photographs of Native Americans everywhere one could be placed. Craft and art and eyes steadied me, as I tottered on the journey toward my tri-racial self.

Everything that was historically repressed in me has hungered to be expressed, to be recognized, to be known. And these three spirits: African, Native American, European, I knew I was bringing to you. In the early days I wrote you a poem about this. And now I wonder if these three spirits were fighting, some of the time I was so depressed. That the Native American and European, no less than the African, desired liberation. Exposure to the light. My sister, who looks more Cherokee and more European than me, tells me the Cherokee great-grandmother from whom we descend was herself mad. She was part African. What did that mean in a tribe that kept slaves and were as colorist, no doubt, as the white settlers who drove them from their homes? I do feel I have had to wrestle with our great-grandmother's spirit and bring it to peace. Which I believe I have done. So that now when I participate in Indian ceremonies I do not feel strange, or a stranger, but exactly who I am, an African-AmerIndian woman with a Native American in her soul. And that I have brought us home.

Collecting the arrowheads from white people who'd found them on their land caused me to think a lot about how empty of Indians Mississippi was. I felt I was walking through a land thick with two- and three-hundred-year-old sorrows, thick with ghosts. Indians are always in my novels because they're always on my mind.

Without their presence the landscape of America seems lonely, speechless. No matter how long we live here, I feel Americans will never know anything about it. In any case, it has been destroyed now beyond knowing.

Last night Harold and I took the kids and we went shopping at that big new supermarket out on Stribling Road. It is a wonderful place. Really huge, and with everything anybody could imagine to want or buy. From grits to lawn chairs. And the best part is that it stays open all night.

So we got our two carts, me and Harold pushing one, the kids pushing the other, and we started down the aisles. Harold makes a real good salary, and he lets us buy anything we want. We bought a gallon of ice cream, after we'd bought all the daily kind of foodstuff.

It was really funny, though, because ordinarily in Mississippi you never see interracial couples. Never. Though you see mixed race children as much as you ever did. Mama says that's not true; she said that, to let her grandmother tell it, it was during slavery that you saw more mixed race children. Those were the ones by the masters that they had off the slave women. They would keep them or sell them, as they saw fit. Then during Reconstruction there were a lot of them because of all the white and black folks who worked together and fell in love, or in lust, or whatever. Anyhow, that's kind of like now, I guess. But what that means is that here in Jackson, if you want to see interracial couples, the place to do it is at midnight at this all-night supermarket.

Folks stare at us so much in the daytime, you start to feel like your skin is crawling. But at midnight there's nobody much at the supermarket. Just the silly clerks, and they're too sleepy to be as mean as they've been brought up to be.

We saw Ruby and Josh, and Ruby's four kids. Josh always looks so outnumbered. Their own baby, Crissy, has light hair, but she's as brown as her mom. And we saw Jerry and Tara; and I think she was drunk. She was wheeling that cart like it was Big Wheels. And then we saw the Lawyer and the Writer. Which is how Harold refers to them. I think he's jealous, myself. He didn't finish law school, and he claims women shouldn't write about themselves.

I asked him Why not? and he said that white male writers, like Faulkner and Hawthorne and Mark Twain, never wrote about themselves, and that they were masters at it. And I asked him whether this didn't come out of a tradition of being a writer but needing to keep quiet about the slaving and gunrunning and Indian killing in your family tree. In other words, I said, if white men wrote truthfully about themselves, how could they continue to fool the rest of us?

Sometimes I make him so mad.

The Lawyer and the Writer had their little chubby baby in their cart. And they were talking to her just like she was as grown as they were. No baby talk at all, and she's still crawling. Do you want us to buy some eggs? they were asking her as we passed them. She said something back, like 'goop,' and they thought that was yes, so they put some eggs next to her.

I think the Writer suspects Harold doesn't care for her. She always speaks real warmly to me; but she leaves her husband the job of saying anything much to Harold. I even think she knows he talks about her. Because one time we ran into them at the picture show—also in the middle of the night—and this was just about the first time we met them, I think. Harold and the Lawyer were making small talk, looking just like two ordinary white men, anywhere. And then when me and the Writer walked back over to them— we'd been to the restroom—Harold turned around to her and said: I hear you're a writer. Kind of smirking, the way he can do. Kind of sniffy. What kind of writer are you? And she looked him up and down and said, real firmly: A shameless one.

The Lawyer couldn't help it. He loved his wife so much, anyhow. But when she said that, he just bust out laughing. His face turned as red as a beet. It is so funny to me that white people turn red like that. You can see all their blood. And she didn't crack a smile, just turned on her boot heel and stalked off to the show. And after the show they were all hugged up on the way home, and the Lawyer was just kissing on her and she was kissing him back and everything about them said: Fuck Mississippi, this is good stuff.

The Ruin

Our Child is trying to figure out where she fit in during those years. Where was she, for instance, when we moved from Mississippi and bought 'the ruin' in Brooklyn.

But here I shall do something I did often when we lived together: veer off into another world. A world of musing, of speculation, of merged fact and fiction. The world of lives glimpsed, but glimpsed to the bone; the world in which one passing word might become a written life.

Do you remember Harold and Dianne? He was blond, from Idaho. She was a local black woman with children. I used to wonder why we were not closer to them; I envied them their raucous and colorful and child-battered household. And I remember that you always commented on the fact that Dianne was 'so humorless' and you wondered what Harold 'saw in her.' One day you said he'd told you: her secret apparently was her expertise at oral sex. I had not warmed to Harold; now I knew why. Although it was Harold who one day said something I've thought about all these years: To stay alive to yourself, you must keep doing the thing that gets you kicked out. He had laughed, saying this. Every choice I make in life he said, to my Republican family, is more abhorrent than the last. They'd almost committed suicide after meeting Dianne.

I could imagine him up there in Idaho, on the family

ranch, six thousand acres wide, his eye pressed against the aperture of the television screen, lusting after the possibility of growing a wider internal, spiritual self that seemed, at the time, to be offered by black and white confrontation in the South. As far as he knew, there were no black people in Idaho, and, curiously, it was his love of the cattle his family raised, his empathy as they were loaded onto boxcars and shipped to a back east market, that made him think the blacks he saw being beaten up on television might be people too.

He was one of the white men who supplied me with arrowheads. It was from his ranch that the tomahawk came. He definitely thought no Indians still lived in Idaho. I think of him whenever I give readings there, and Indians, some of them friends of mine, claim front-row seats.

Harold and Dianne are both dead now.

At a reading in Oxford, a shy son and daughter came up to me. I was busy hugging on Ned Bing, the indomitable white pastor whose house was firebombed and whose face was badly battered by members of the Klan. It had been years since we'd seen each other. He has no idea how much I love his face; and I didn't tell him, as I should have, as we stood surrounded by half the town. However I did manage to kiss him just where they'd laid open his jaw, and I pulled on the big, bright pink ear that was stitched back on halfheartedly at the racist hospital, and that managed, out of sheer love, to hang on. And then I stepped back, and there they were, the grown children of Harold and Dianne. Black children, because she'd had them by someone else, some black high school sweetheart, long before Harold arrived. Big brown eyes, dimpled smiles, skin like warm silk. Hair in dreads.

We are the children of Harold and Dianne, they said in unison. Clearly a line rehearsed, since they'd anticipated being shy in front of me. Goddess, I thought, who are they talking about. And please ma'am, I pleaded with Her, let me soon remember. They were that impressive. I wanted to be worthy of them. My face, you always said, was completely readable. It must have been so then, as I rummaged through my Mississippi memory bank, because they laughed. Bust out laughing, in fact. And I saw Dianne's lips, her rarely glimpsed dimple—and realized she'd almost never smiled—and what her hair would have looked like if she'd ceased to straighten it, and just let it grow. I even saw, especially in the boy, some of Harold's supercilious cockiness. The way, in Mississippi, he seemed arrogant even just standing on a corner. He was a hard white man for blacks to cotton to, so to speak. Ah, I said, seeing now what he might have looked like as a black man, and opened my arms.

They flowed into me, both of them, in an embrace that seemed to last forever. They flopped and draped, one to a shoulder, about my body, which met them as if it were a tree. Not a stiff tree, but one that just bends to the ground when there's a wind. A weeping willow. Do you ever wonder, old lover of mine, where so much love comes from? I wonder this often, because no matter how distressing the world is, wherever I am, there never seems to be a shortage of love. Is this true, as well, for you? We hugged for so long, in fact, that Reverend Bing returned, and gathered the three of us close to him.

Maybe the love is there because of shared suffering? Maybe it rises up wherever we perceive that another human has survived. As human. In any case, the three of us left the throng that had filled the reading venue and went next door to a café that specialized in fried oysters and grits. The food was bad when we lived in Mississippi. Remember? We used to drive all the way to New Orleans, a four-hour trip, just to eat decent food once a month. But here, in the town of Oxford, a bicycle ride from Rowan Oak, Faulkner's old plantation house, the food is exquisite, and I stuffed myself with oysters, while thinking of my father, whose taste buds I seem to have inherited, and who adored oysters, raw, stewed or fried.

Ernesto and Rosa ate heartily. I would not have guessed tragedy was such a part of their life, if they had not hugged me so deeply, as if my body were a kind of raft.

You are one of the few people who knew our parents,

said Rosa, after explaining that both she and Ernesto were completing degrees at the university.

We lost them, you know. Said Ernesto.

No, I said. I don't know.

Reverend Bing looked at me quizzically. I shrugged. I have dropped out of so much of the world that I am aware I miss news I should have heard. Did you know of their deaths? Did you read about it in the paper? Did someone tell you? I pushed away the remains of my lavishly buttered grits.

Nowadays, when everywhere you look there is so much tragedy, so much sadness, whenever I am about to hear more of it, I scrutinize the person or persons who are about to speak. I am looking to see if they are still beautiful, regardless of the tale they are about to tell. And if they are still beautiful, before they say anything, I tell them that they are. This is because Greatness of Beauty is how I see God. God being the common name given by many people to that which is undeniably unsurpassable, obvious and true.

You could not be more beautiful, I said to them. And this is so.

Did you know that Dianne wanted to be a writer? I had no idea.

But that was the first thing Rosa told me. Ernesto chimed in to say that Harold had not permitted her to publish anything. Blinking a bit nervously he said Dianne had spoken admiringly of my work, but that Harold had ridiculed it. He thought, said Rosa, that because you wrote about your own life, that you were shameless. He was terrified to think our mother would write about herself.

And now we know why, said Ernesto.

Yeah, said Rosa, thowing her napkin over her plate.

You have always pestered me to tell you where I was the night before I moved in with you.

This first line from Dianne's diary conjured up her face for me. It is a funny line, no? A great opening statement for the novel she might have written, had Harold let her.

How did I end up living with a white man from Idaho? The first time I saw you I hated your guts. I thought all blond people were stupid and that white skin looked diseased. We were taught that white people smell funny. Like wet dogs. But thank the Lord you didn't have blue eyes, those hard glass eyes that might as well be playing marbles, and never show emotion and never even show fear. And you were busy trying to teach people how to vote and being impatient because, in their fear of you as a white man, they had a hard time hearing anything you had to say. If you'd cursed them and called them dumb niggers they would have heard you perfectly. But you were so polite, even while impatient, and called them Sir and Ma'am, and you just about shocked them out of their clothes.

What was kissing you like, the first time? I remember feeling fear, because I was thinking Good Lord, where are this man's lips? What must have happened to them? I mean long ago, maybe when the earth's climate or something changed. I have kissed a lot of men in my life, and they all had lips, sometimes more than enough lips to tell you the truth. But kissing you I felt my mouth just kind of spreading all over your face looking for lips to match up to mine. I was seriously worried that I was blocking your nose. But you just kept going ummm, ummm, ummm, and pretty soon I quit worrying about it.

Who would have thought? That very morning my daddy had reminded me that white men are lower than snakes. But he wasn't too high off the ground his own self. And the black men who fathered my children didn't exactly fly among the clouds. Still, it was with a black man, the father of one of my children, that I spent the last night of my life as a pure black woman. He was out on bail, or maybe he'd run away from the jail, black men often did; and he'd come to see me and the children and one thing led to another. He was the one my mama always liked; you know how mothers sometimes be. And she came by, just as nice, and took all the children over to her house. And Daniel and me just fell in the bed together and hugged each other a long time and just started crying. And he asked me if it was true that I was *going out with a white man, and I said yes. And he asked me if I thought he and I could ever get together again, even though he was set to go to prison for twenty-something years, and I said I didn't think so. And then he asked me if he could spend the night. And I said no. But then we cried so much we tired ourselves out and went to sleep. And then around midnight we woke up, and just started to make love. And we made love over and over for the next six or seven hours, until the children came back and he had to leave.*

The next night I moved in with you. And I wouldn't make love with you because I could still smell Daniel in my body. And the next night I said I had my period. And when we finally did make love, I felt like I had just given up.

Every time you got mad with me about something, you always yelled that I didn't really love you. I think it upset you that all my children were so dark. But you felt like this because until you were twenty-seven years old the thought of a black person's life never entered your head. It was news to you that us poor black folks down in Mississippi had even survived. You thought we were just like the Indians you said no longer existed in Idaho. Sometimes, even when you were looking me straight in my face, I could see you were still surprised. I used to think I should gain a lot of weight and put on a head rag to make you feel more at home.

I knew you were jealous of black men. And envious at the same time. You'd heard things about black men, growing up. Sexual things, that made you feel inferior. And after you saw a picture of Daniel in the newspaper, after he'd escaped from prison and was thought to be hiding out in New York City, you were evil for weeks. I was happy he'd got away. Every day of my life it hurt me to think of him in a cage. But you never understood about prison in the South. That prisons were just the modern version of the plantation. That if someone like Daniel stole something because he was hungry, he shouldn't be forced to work cotton for the rest of his life.

I feel somehow embarrassed, reading Dianne's diary. I protested when Ernesto and Rosa (after Ernesto Che Guevara and Rosa Parks, of course) sent it to me. At first, I wouldn't even open it; I was almost afraid. Afraid of what? Of seeing the writing self, my own, that might not have become. After all, there we all were, in Mississippi, at the same time, encountering the same violence, racism, sweltering heat. Only you supported me in the work I chose to do in the world. Harold did not support Dianne; though he was, apparently, a good father to her children. Whenever I think of Ernesto I actually see Harold; the way he used to stand, legs spread, his arms folded across his chest, his glasses pushed up on his head, glinting in the sun atop his turbulent blond hair.

No, no, she wanted you to read what she was writing, even while she was writing it and you lived a few miles away! She was desperate for someone to share her writing with. This is what the children tell me. Rosa is herself thinking of writing a novel, just because Dianne never could. Ernesto thinks perhaps he will be a journalist for television.

I sat in bed with the diary after it arrived. It is not like my journals, which are sequential, systematic, by years. It is not even finished, and is haphazard. Dianne's thoughts are jotted down raw, just as they came to her, with no attempt to mold them into anything other than what she actually felt at the time. A diary like this, with so many blank pages, seems to reflect a life permeated with gaps, an existence full of holes. But perhaps that is what happens when one's experience is so intensely different from anything dreamed of as a child that there seems literally to be no words for it. For living with a white man, and having him be, somehow, in brutal Mississippi, an exemplary father to her black children, must have seemed to Dianne stranger than any childhood fantasy she might have had.

I used to feel that way, myself. Though what I've come to realize about myself is that I honestly like living on the edge, wherever it is; that is where I feel most alive and most free. And so I cherished the strangeness of us; and sometimes as we sat down to eat breakfast together, I looked at you across the table and thought you might as well have been a leopard lying waiting for prey on the limb of a tree. Strange, maybe dangerous, but so exciting and beautiful!

But back to 'the ruin.'

Your mother did not understand the concept of 'Brownstoning.' Buying a dilapidated row house in the wilds of Brooklyn and transforming it into a comfortable and spacious home. Why we thought she'd get it, and give us a favorable report on the house we'd chosen by photograph sent to us by a Brooklyn realtor, I know not. The exquisitely remodeled, light-filled triplex, three doors from Prospect Park, in the very best part of Park Slope, she told us was in a slum. What did we know? Essentially, what did I know? Sleepwalking through the heat of our last Jackson, Mississippi summer, subsisting of bicycle rides and Valium, I knew only what I read in the few books on brownstoning I'd managed to buy on trips to New York. Your mother was born and raised in Brooklyn, as you were. I thought her opinion held water, until, months later, I saw with my own eyes the house she'd encouraged us not to buy. The most perfect house in Brooklyn.

Instead, with time running out for us in Mississippi, and New York once again calling, we found ourselves with one week in which to house shop. And chose a beautiful but literal ruin, on a calm, out of the way street in Brooklyn, that it would take a year to get completely clean, and nearly three to renovate.

Our blood went into that house. And the last shred of the love that had so characterized our life. The plumbing alone cost every cent you received from the sale of your share of your law firm. Every word I wrote was transformed into lighting fixtures, doorknobs and paint. We were not wise enough to know not to try to live in this foolishness. We did not know we should have done something else. At times like this, I felt our isolation most keenly. That we lacked parents or friends who would say: Look how tired you both are. It's obvious. Sell the law firm, yes, but take the money and go to Negril for six months. Write from a resort in the Rocky Mountains, if write you must, and save the money to live on the Upper West Side in New York, in a part of town already renovated. Enough, already! You don't have to keep challenging and 'improving' the world by avoiding yourselves! For we did learn to avoid ourselves, avoid each other. Our pitiful attempt to avoid our failure, avoid our pain.

The night before we decided to buy the ruin we'd stayed at your mother's house. She had magnanimously given us her bed. But as I sat on the edge of the bed, after putting Our Child to sleep next door, in your old room, she came in, and warned me not to put anything on her dresser because whatever I put there—hairbrush or whatever—might scratch the finish. And I knew I could not sleep in her bed. And so I went, lucky for us we'd been given the keys until we made up our minds, straight to 'the ruin.' And slept alone on the floor, during what turned out to be my first night in the new house.

We were so far apart by then I would not have wanted
you to come with me. Still, I missed your nearness, in the
strange, gloomy house, in which only a few lights on the
first floor, and a couple on the fourth floor, worked. It
was a house with eight fireplaces! Were we hoping for
warmth and coziness, or what?

But it was not to be. Not for the two of us, who, in the
enormous house, passed each other like ships in the
night. You went each day to a law office in midtown
Manhattan, far away from the clients in Mississippi
whose slow, drawling comments and stories you loved,
and who sometimes paid you with fried chicken and
watermelons. I could see your deep unhappiness to be
back in the city you'd so eagerly left. Seeking to ignore
my own disorientation, I learned everything there was to
know about fireplace tile and floor varnish and grout.
Twice a week I went into the city to work for a women's
magazine. I had anxiety attacks of such severity I thought
I would, one day, simply fail to arrive at my destination.
For several years, I often felt as though I were floating
through the streets of Brooklyn and New York. And that
you were somewhere out there, too, but I felt little
connection to you.

But Our Child seemed happy. She had friends her own
age up and down our street. She loved her school and her
teachers. She had a baby-sitter across from us who was
from the Islands and taught her to make wonderful

simple food, like *aroz con pollo*, her favorite dish. This I say now, to her, in her therapist's office, as she sits, pensively, all five feet six of her, leaning slightly forward, and, I am sad to note, silently weeping. How odd it feels to realize she could not have known, although perhaps she did, being so sensitive, the pain and sorrow that was so heavy in our hearts. That perhaps we were not dragging around the house in her child's mind, as we were dragging around it in our own.

And now, beloved, it seems to me that our major fault, all these years, is that we never took the time before, any of us, to properly grieve what we lost. What *we*, as a perky little human family in a frighteningly unloving culture and country, lost, when our small dream of an indomitable love ended. And this is in addition to the fact that we also failed to properly mourn the deaths by assassination and terrorism of so many people in public life whom we admired and loved, because to do so would have simply overwhelmed us. We would have given up and died. Maybe the beginning of our end as a couple was the day when we learned Martin had been killed and I promptly miscarried. How will anyone ever understand how much we loved him?

Even today I can barely bring myself to listen to his voice. At times I force myself to do so. And sure enough, after thinking that my heart will break one more unendurable time, he resolutely pulls me through the pain. He left us on such a high note of fearlessness and hope. Maybe he lied to us, though. Maybe there is no 'promised land' for us. Just look at this poor country, like the orphan of the Universe. But even this fails to frighten me anymore. I believe only the moment we are in is promised, and that it, whatever it is, should always be 'the future' we want.

And that is why I am thinking of you, and reminding you of a moment in which we, unlikely us, shared a vision and a reality of love, that need not be completely lost. If North America survives, it will not look like or be like it is today. One day there will be, created out of all of us lovers, an American race—remember how Jean Toomer, whom we sometimes read to each other, in Mississippi, was already talking about this American race, even in the Thirties? We will simply not let the writers of history claim we did not exist. Why should the killers of the world be 'the future' and not us?

Kindred Spirits

Rosa could not tell her sister how scared she was or how glad she was that she had consented to come with her. Instead they made small talk on the plane, and Rosa looked out of the window at the clouds.

It was a kind of sentimental journey for Rosa, months too late, going to visit the aunt in whose house their grandfather had died. She did not even know why she must do it: she had spent the earlier part of the summer in such far-flung places as Cyprus and Greece. Jamaica. She was at a place in her life where she seemed to have no place. She'd left the brownstone in Park Slope, given up the car and cat. Her child was at camp. She was in pain. That, at least, she knew. She hardly slept. If she did sleep, her dreams were cold, desolate, and full of static.

She ate spaghetti, mostly, with shrimp, from a recipe cut out from the *Times*. She listened to the jazz radio station all the time, her heart in her mouth.

'So how is Ivan?' her sister, Barbara, said.

Barbara was still fond of her brother-in-law, and hurt that after his divorce from Rosa he'd sunk back into the white world so completely that even a Christmas card was too much trouble to send people who had come to love him.

'Oh, fine,' Rosa said. 'Living with a nice Jewish girl, at last.' Which might have explained the absence of a Christmas card, Rosa thought, but she knew it really didn't.

'Really? What's she like?'

'Warm. Attractive. Loves him.'

This was mostly guesswork on Rosa's part; she'd met her only once. She hoped she had these attributes, for his sake. A week after she'd moved out of the brownstone Sheila had moved in, and all her in-laws, especially Ivan's mother, seemed very happy. Once she'd 'borrowed' the car (her own, which she'd left with him) and when she returned it mother and girlfriend met her at her own front gate, barring her way into her own house, their faces flushed with the victory of finally seeing her outside where she belonged. Music and the laughter of many guests came from inside.

But did she care? No. She was free. She took to the sidewalk, the heels of her burgundy suede boots clicking, free. Her heart making itself still by force. Ah, but then at night when she slept, it awoke, and the clicking of her heels was nothing to the rattling and crackling of her heart.

'Mama misses him,' said Barbara.

Rosa knew she did. How could she even begin to understand that this son-in-law she doted on was incapable, after divorcing her daughter, of even calling on the phone to ask how she felt, as she suffered stroke after frightening and debilitating stroke? It must have seemed totally unnatural to her, a woman who had rushed to comfort the 'sick and shut-in' all her life, as it did, actually, to Rosa, who about most other things was able to take a somewhat more modern view.

At last they were in sight of the Miami airport. Before they could be prevented by the stewardess Barbara and Rosa managed to exchange seats. Barbara sat by the window because she flew very rarely and it was a treat for her to 'see herself' landing. Rosa no longer cared to look down. She had traveled so much that summer. The trip to Cyprus in particular had been so long it had made her want to scream. And then, in Nicosia, the weather was abominable. 120 degrees. It hurt to breathe. And there had been days of visiting Greeks in refugee camps and listening to socialists and visiting the home of a family in which an only son—standing next to a socialist leader at a rally—was assassinated by mistake. Though it had happened over a year earlier his father still wept as he told of it, and looked with regret at his surviving daughter and *her* small daughter. 'A man must have many sons,' he said over and over, never seeming to realize that under conditions of war even a dozen sons could be killed. And not under war alone.

And then Rosa had flown to Greece, and Athens had been like New York City in late July and the Parthenon tiny...

When they arrived in the Miami airport they looked about with the slightly anxious interest of travelers who still remembered segregated travel facilities. If a white person had materialized beside them and pointed out a colored section they would have attacked him or her on principle, but been only mildly surprised. Their formative years had been lived under racist restrictions so pervasive that wherever they traveled in the world they expected, on some level in themselves and in whatever physical circumstances they found themselves, to encounter some, if only symbolic, racial barrier.

And there it was now: On a poster across from them a blonde white woman and her dark-haired male partner danced under the stars while a black band played and a black waiter waited and a black chef beamed from the kitchen.

A striking woman in a blue pastel cotton dress, tall, straight of bearing, black as midnight with a firm bun of silver white hair, bore down upon them.

'It's me,' thought Rosa, 'my old self.'

'Aunt Lily!' said Barbara, smiling, and throwing her arms around her.

When it was her turn to be hugged, Rosa gave herself up to it, enjoying the smells of baby shampoo, Jergens lotion and Evening in Paris remembered from childhood embraces, and which, on second sniff, she decided was all Charlie. That was this aunt, full of change and contradictions, as she had known her.

Not that she ever had, really. Aunt Lily had come to visit summers, when she was a child. She had been straight and black and as vibrant as fire. She was always with her husband, whose tan face seemed weak next to hers. He drove the car, but she steered it; the same seemed true of their lives.

They had moved to Florida years ago, looking for a better life 'somewhere else in the South that wasn't so full of Southerners.' Finding 'good white people' to work for had seemed Aunt Lily's talent. Though looking at her now, Rosa thought her aunt, by her imperial bearing, directness of speech and great height, had probably made them so. She could not imagine anyone having the nerve to condescend to Aunt Lily, or, worse, attempt to cheat her. And so, once again she was amazed at the white man's arrogance and racist laws. Ten years earlier this sweet-smelling, squeaky-clean aunt of hers would not have been permitted to try on a dress in local department stores. She could not have drunk at certain fountains. The main restaurants of the city would have been closed to her. The public library. The vast majority of the city's toilets.

Aunt Lily had an enormous brown station wagon into which Rosa and Barbara flung their light travel bags. Barbara, older than Rosa and closer to Aunt Lily, sat beside her on the front seat. Rosa sat behind them, looking out the window at the passing scenery, admiring the numerous canals—she was passionately fond of water—and yet wondering about the city's sewerage problems, of which she had heard.

How like them, really, she thought, to build canals around their pretty segregated houses that are so polluted that to fall into one was to risk disease.

When they arrived at Aunt Lily's squat green house with its orange and lemon trees in the yard, far from canals and even street lights, they were met in the narrow hall by five of her aunt's seven foster children and a young woman who had been a foster child herself but was now sharing the house and helping to look after the children with Aunt Lily. Her name was Raymyna Ann.

*

Aunt Lily had, a long time ago, a baby son who died. For years she had not seemed to care for children; Rosa had never felt particularly valued by her whenever she'd come to visit. Aunt Lily acknowledged her brother's children by bringing them oranges and grapefruit packed in orange net bags. She rarely hugged or kissed them. Well, she rarely touched these foster children, either, Rosa noticed. There were so many of them, so dark (all as black, precisely, as her aunt) and so woundedly silent. But at dinner the table was piled high with food, the little ones were encouraged to have seconds, and when they all trooped off to bed they did so in a cloud of soapy smells and dazzling linen.

Rosa lay in the tiny guest room, which had been her grandfather's room, and smoked a cigarette. Aunt Lily's face appeared at the door.

'Now, Rosa, I don't allow smoking or drinking in my house.'

Rosa rose from the bed to put her cigarette out. Her aunt watching her as if she were a child.

'*You* used to smoke and drink,' she said, piqued at her aunt's self-righteous tone.

'Your mama told you that lie,' said Aunt Lily, unsmiling. 'She was always trying to say I was fast. But I never did drink. I tried to, and it made me sick. Every time she said she didn't want me laying on her freshly made up bed drunk, I wasn't drunk, I was sick.'

'Oh,' said Rosa, who had the unfortunate tendency of studying people very closely when they spoke. It occurred to her for the first time that Aunt Lily didn't like her mother.

But *why* didn't Aunt Lily like her mother? The question nagged at her that night as she tried to sleep. Then became lost in the many other questions that presented themselves, well into the dawn.

Why, for instance, did Ivan no longer like her? And how could you live with someone for over a decade and 'love' them, then, as soon as you were no longer married, you didn't even like them?

Her marriage had been wonderful, she felt. Only the divorce was horrible.

The most horrible thing of all was losing Ivan's friendship and comradely support, which he yanked out of her reach with a vengeance that sent her reeling. Two weeks after the divorce became final she was in the hospital for surgery that proved to have been minor only after the fact. He neither called nor sent a note.

Sheila, now his wife, wouldn't have liked it, he later (years later) explained.

And she had said, by then:

'Who? *Who* wouldn't have liked it?'

And he had had to remind her who Sheila was. This

was not because her memory was so poor—it actually was poor—but because he no longer called his wife by name but by some more generic 'mother/housefrau' appellation made up after their babies started to come.

The next day all the children were in school and Barbara stood behind Aunt Lily's chair combing and braiding her long silver hair. Rosa sat on the couch looking at them. Raymyna busily vacuumed the bedroom floors, popping in occasionally to bring the mail or a glass of water. She was getting married in a couple of weeks and would be moving out to start her own family. Rosa had of course not said anything when she heard this, but her inner response was surprise. She could not easily comprehend anyone getting married, now that she no longer was, but it was impossible for her to feel happy at the prospect of yet another poor black woman marrying God knows who and starting a family. She would have thought Raymyna had already had enough.

But who was she to talk. Miss Cynical. She had married. And enjoyed it. She had had a child, and adored it.

In the afternoon her aunt and Raymyna took them sightseeing. As she understood matters from the local newspapers, all the water she saw—whether canal, river or ocean—was polluted beyond recall, so that it was hard even to look at it, much less to look at it admiringly. She could only gaze at it in sympathy. The beach she also found pitiable. In their attempt to hog it away from the poor, the black and the locals in general, the beachfront 'developers' had erected massive boxlike hotels that blocked the view of the water for all except those rich enough to pay for rooms on the beach side of the hotels. Through the cracks between hotels Rosa saw the mostly elderly sunworshipers walking along what seemed to be a pebbly, eroded beach, stretching out their poor white necks to the sun.

Of course they cruised through 'little Havana', which stretched for miles. Rosa looked at the new Cuban immigrants (*gusanos*, Fidel called them, worms) with interest. Startled that already they seemed as a group to live better and to have more material goods than the black people. Like many Americans who supported the Cuban revolution she found the Cubans who left Cuba somewhat less noble than the ones who'd stayed. Clearly the ones who'd left were the ones with money. Hardly anyone in Cuba could afford the houses, the cars, the clothes, the television sets and lawnmowers she saw.

At dinner she tried to explain why and how she had missed her grandfather's funeral. The telegram had come the evening before she left for Cyprus. As she left her stoop next morning she had felt herself heading in the wrong direction. But she could not stop. It had taken all her meager energy to plan the trip to Cyprus, with a friend who claimed it was beautiful, and she simply could not think to change her plans. Nor could she, still bearing the wounds of her separation from Ivan, face her family, so many, perhaps all, of whom had been uncomfortable with him anyway.

Barbara and Aunt Lily listened to her patiently. It didn't surprise her that neither knew where Cyprus was, or what its politics and history were. She told them about the man whose son was killed and how he seemed to hate his 'worthless' daughter for being alive.

'Women are not valued in their culture,' she explained. 'In fact, the Greeks, the Turks and the Cyprians have this one thing in common, though they fight over everything else. The father kept saying "A man should have many sons." His wife flinched guiltily when he said it.'

'After Ma died, I went and got my father,' Aunt Lily was saying. 'And I told him, no smoking and drinking in my house.'

But her grandfather had always smoked. He smoked a pipe. She'd liked the smell of it.

'And no cardplaying and no noise and no complaining because I don't want to hear it.'

Others of her brothers and sisters had come to see

him. She had been afraid to. On the pictures she saw, he always looked happy. But when he was not dead tired or drunk, happy was how he'd looked. A deeply silent man with those odd peaceful eyes—she did not know, and she was confident her aunt didn't, what he really thought about anything. So he had stopped smoking, her aunt thought, but her brothers had always slipped him tobacco. He had stopped drinking. That was possible. Even before his wife, Rosa's grandmother, had died he had given up liquor. Or, as he said 'it had given him up.' So, no noise. Little company. No complaining. But he wasn't the complaining type, was he? He liked best of all, Rosa thought, to be left alone. And he liked baseball. She felt he had liked her too. She hoped he did. But never did he say so. And he was so stingy! In her whole life he'd only given her fifteen cents. On the other hand, he'd financed her sister Barbara's trade school education, which her father, his son, had refused to do.

Was that what she held against him on the flight away from the South, toward the Middle East? There was no excuse, she'd known it all the time. She needed to be there, to say goodbye to the spiritcase. For wasn't she beginning to understand the appearance of his spiritcase as her own spirit struggled and suffered?

At night, massaging Barbara's thin shoulders before turning in, she looked into her own face reflected in the bureau mirror. She was beginning to have the look her grandfather had when he was very, very tired. The look he got just before something broke in him and he went on a mind-killing drunk. It was there in her eyes. So clearly. The look of abandonment. Of having no support. Of loneliness so severe every minute was a chant against self-destruction.

She massaged Barbara but she knew her touch was that of a stranger. At what point, she wondered, did you lose connection with people you loved? And she remembered going to visit Barbara when she was in college and Barbara lived a short bus ride away. And she was present when Barbara's husband beat her and called her names and once he had locked both of them out of the house overnight. And her sister called the police and they seemed nice to Rosa, so recently up from the South, but in fact they were bored and cynical as they listened to Barbara's familiar complaint. Rosa was embarrassed and couldn't believe anything so sordid could be happening to them, so respected was their family in the small town they were from. But, in any event, Barbara continued to live with her husband many more years, and Rosa was so hurt and angry she wanted to kill. But most of all, she was disappointed in Barbara, who threw herself into the inevitable weekend battles with passionately vulgar language that Rosa had never heard any woman, not to mention her gentle sister, use before. Her sister's spirit seemed polluted to her, so much so that the sister she had known as a child seemed gone altogether. And once gone, she had never come back.

Was disappointment, then, the hardest thing to bear? Or was it the consciousness of being powerless to change things, to help? And certainly she had been very conscious of that. As he punched out her sister, Rosa had almost felt the blows on her body. But she had not flung herself between them wielding a butcher knife as she had done once when Barbara was being attacked by their father, another raving madman.

Barbara had wanted to go to their brother's grammar school graduation. Their father had insisted that she go to the funeral of an elderly church mother instead. Barbara had tried to refuse. But *crack*, he had slapped her across the face. She was sixteen, plump and lovely. Rosa adored her. She ran immediately to get the knife, but she was so small no one seemed to notice her, wedging herself between them. But had she been larger and stronger she might have killed him; for even as a child she was serious in all she did—and then what would her life, the life of a murderer, have been like? Thinking of that day she wept. At her love, her sister's anguish. Barbara had been forced to go to the funeral, the print of her father's fingers hidden by powder and rouge.

*

She was little and weak and she did not understand what was going on anyway between father and sister. To her, her father acted like he was jealous. And in college, after such a long struggle to get there, how could she stab her brother-in-law to death without killing her future, herself? And so she had lain on her narrow foldaway cot in the tiny kitchen in the stuffy apartment over the laundromat and had listened to the cries and whispers, the pummelings, the screams and pleas. And then, still awake, she listened to the silibant sounds of 'making up,' harder to bear and to understand than the fights.

She had not killed for her sister. (And one would have had to kill the mindless drunken brutalizing husband, a blow to the head might only have made him more angry.) Her guilt soon clouded over the love, and around Barbara she retreated into a silence that she realized was very like her grandfather's. The sign of disappointment hinged to powerlessness. A thoughtful black man in the racist early twentieth-century South, he probably could have told her a thing or two about the squeaking of the hinge. But had he? No. He'd only complained about his wife, and so convincingly that for a time Rosa, like everyone else in the family, lost respect for her. It seemed her problem was that she was not mentally quick, and because she stayed with him even as he said this Rosa and her relatives were moved to agree. Yet there was nowhere else she could have gone. Perhaps her grandfather had found the house in which they lived, but she, her grandmother, had made it a home. Once the grandmother died, the house seemed empty, though he remained behind.

Aunt Lily was handing out the remaining odds and ends of her grandfather's things. Barbara got the trunk, that magic repository of tobacco and candy when they were children. Rosa received a small shaving mirror with a gilt lion on its back. There were several of the large, white 'twenty-five-cent hanskers' her grandfather had used. The granddaughters received half a dozen each. That left only her grandfather's hats. One brown and one gray, old, worn, none too clean fedoras. She knew Barbara was far too fastidious to want them. Rosa placed one on her head. She loved how she looked—she looked like him—in it.

It was killing her, how much she loved him. And he'd been so mean to her grandmother, and so stingy, too. Once he had locked her out of the house because she had bought herself a penny stick of candy from the grocery money.

But then when Rosa knew him he had been beautiful. Peaceful, mystical almost in his silences and calm, and she realized he was imprinted on her heart just that way. It really did not seem fair.

To check her tears she turned to Aunt Lily.

'Tell me what my father was like as a boy,' she said.

Her aunt looked at her, she felt, with hatred.

'You should have asked him when he was alive.'

Rosa looked about for Barbara who had disappeared into the bathroom. By now she was weeping openly. Her aunt looking at her impassively.

'I don't want to find myself in anything you write. And you can just leave your daddy alone too.'

She could not remember whether she'd ever asked her father about his life. But surely she had, since she knew quite a lot. She turned and walked into the bathroom, forgetful that she was thirty-five, her sister forty-one, and that you can only walk in on your sister in the toilet if you are both children. But it didn't matter. Barbara had always been accessible, always protective. Rosa remembered one afternoon when she was five or six, she and Barbara and a cousin of theirs about Barbara's age set out on an errand. They were walking silently down the dusty road when a large car driven by a white man nearly ran them down. His car sent up billows of dust from the dirt road that stung their eyes and stained their clothes. Instinctively Rosa had picked up a fistful of sand from the road and thrown it after him. He stopped the car, backed it up furiously and slammed on the brakes, getting out next to them, three black, barefoot girls who looked at him as only they could. Was he a human being? Or a devil? At any rate he had seen Rosa throw the sand, he said, and he wanted the older girls to warn her against doing such things 'for the little nigger's own good.'

Rosa would have admitted throwing the sand. After all, the man had seen her.

But—'She didn't throw no sand,' said Barbara, quietly, striking a heavy womanish pose with both hands on her hips.

'She did so,' said the man, his face red from heat and anger.

'She didn't,' said Barbara.

The cousin simply stared at the man. After all, what was a small handful of sand compared to the billows of sand with which he'd covered them?

Cursing, the man stomped into his car, and drove off.

For a long time it had seemed to Rosa that only black people were always in danger. But there was also the sense that her big sister would know how to help them out of it.

But now, as her sister sat on the commode, Rosa saw a look on her face that she had never seen before, and she realized her sister had heard what Aunt Lily said. It was a look that said she'd got the reply she deserved. For wasn't she always snooping about the family's business and turning things about in her writing in ways that made the family shudder? There was no talking to her as you talked to regular people. The minute you opened your mouth a meter went on. Rosa could read all this on her sister's face. She didn't need to speak. And it was a lonely feeling that she had. For Barbara was right. Aunt Lily too. And she could no more stop the meter running than she could stop her breath. An odd look across the room fifteen years ago still held the power to make her wonder about it, try to 'decipher' or at least understand it. This was her curse: never to be able to forget, truly, but only to appear to forget. And then to record what she could not forget.

Suddenly, in her loneliness, she laughed.

'He was a recorder with his eyes,' she said, under her breath. For it seemed to her she'd penetrated her grandfather's serenity, his frequent silences. The meter had ticked in him too; he too was all attentiveness. But for him that had had to be enough; she'd rarely seen him with a pencil in his hand; she thought he'd only had one or two years of school. She imagined him 'writing' stories during his long silences merely by thinking them, not embarrassing other people with them, as she did.

She had been obsessed by this old man whom she so definitely resembled. And now, perhaps, she knew why.

We were kindred spirits, she thought, as she sat, one old dusty fedora on her head, the other in her lap, on the plane home. But in a lot of ways, before I knew him, he was a jerk.

She thought of Ivan. For it was something both of them had said often about their relationship: that though he was white and she was black they were in fact kindred spirits. And she had thought so, until the divorce, after which his spirit became as unfathomable to her as her grandfather's would have been before she knew him. But perhaps Ivan, too, was simply acting like a jerk?

She felt, as she munched dry crackers and cheese the pert stewardess brought, in the very wreckage of her life. She had not really looked at Barbara since that moment in the toilet, when it became clear to her how her sister really perceived her. She knew she would not see Aunt Lily again and that if Aunt Lily died before she herself did she would not go to her funeral. Nor would she ever, ever write about her. She took a huge swallow of ginger ale and tried to drown out the incessant ticking...

She stroked the soft felt of her grandfather's hat, thought of how peculiarly the human brain grows from an almost invisible seed, and how, in this respect, it was rather similar to understanding, a process it engendered. She looked into the shaving mirror and her eyes told her she could bear very little more. She felt herself begin to slide into the long silence in which such thoughts would be her sole companions. Maybe she would even find happiness in it.

But then, just when she was almost gone, Barbara put on their grandfather's other hat, and reached for her hand.

Orelia and John

Olive Oil

She was busy cooking dinner, a nice ratatouille, chopping and slicing eggplant, zucchini and garlic. George Winston was on the box and the fire crackled in the stove. As she dripped olive oil into a pan a bit of it stuck to her thumb and she absentmindedly used her rather rough forefinger to rub it into the cuticle, which she noticed was also cracked. In fact, she had worked a lot over the last month putting in a winter garden; the weather most days had been mild, but it was also dry and occasionally there had been wind. Hence the extreme dryness of the skin on her hands.

Thinking of this, puttering about, putting a log on the fire and a pot of water for noodles on the stove, she touched her face, which, along her cheekbones, seemed to rustle it was so dry. Massaging the painfully dry cuticle, she swooped up the bottle of olive oil, sniffed it for freshness, and poured a tablespoonful into her hand. Rubbing her hands together she rubbed the oil all over her neck and face. Then she rubbed it into wrists, arms and legs as well.

When John came in from splitting wood he sniffed the air hopefully, wanting to enjoy the smell of the ratatouille, one of his favorite dishes. Putting the wood down and kissing Orelia on the cheek he noticed how bright, almost burnished her skin looked. He was sorry he had a cold and could not smell her, since her sweet fresh smell always delighted him.

'Still can't smell anything, eh?' she asked.

'Nope.'

To which she replied, emphatically, 'Good.'

One of the sad things about their relationship was that even though she loved John she was unable to expect the best from him. John sometimes thought this was solely his fault, but it wasn't. Orelia had been brought up in a family and a society in which men did not frequently *do* their best in relation to women, but rather a kind of exaggerated approximation of what their male peers told them was correct. Then, too, at a very young age, when she was no more than seven, her older brother, Raymond, gentle and loving, whom she had adored, betrayed her. Her other brothers, insensitive and wild, had designated an ugly, derisive nickname for her, 'Rhino' (because even as a little girl dryness caused the skin on elbows and knees to appear gray and thick), which she had borne as well as she could until one day he called her by it. She was shattered and never again really trusted a man not to unexpectedly and obliviously hurt her feelings no matter how much she loved him.

So John was not trusted, no matter what he did, and sometimes he pointed this out to her, but mostly he kept quiet. No matter how many times he proved himself different from other men, in her eyes he always seemed to measure up just the same, and this was depressing. However, he loved Orelia and understood many of the ways she had been hurt by society and her family and empathized with her.

While they were eating he mentioned how glowing she looked and she simply smiled and forked up bowls of salad. He was surprised she didn't tell him immediately what she had done to herself—that was her usual way.

That night before she went to bed she washed herself from face to feet in the tin washbasin he had bought, a feat that regularly amazed him because she did, indeed, manage to get clean in less than a half gallon of water, whereas John felt the need each night to fire up the wood-burning hot water heater and luxuriate under a hot shower that used gallons. While he bathed in the bathhouse outside, she went wild in the kitchen with the olive oil, massaging it into her scalp, between her braids, into her face and body, into her feet. Glowing like a lamp she preceeded a bewitched John up the narrow ladder to the sleeping loft.

Alas, the day must soon come when John got back his sense of smell; his colds rarely lasted longer than a week. Orelia thought about this every day as she slathered on the olive oil. She had grown to love the stuff. Unlike her various sweet-smelling oils and creams it really combatted and won the battle over her skin's excessive dryness, and its purity brought the glow of honest health to her skin.

Orelia and John had been intimate for so long that any little secret kept from him was like a sharp piece of straw in his sock. One night when the worst of his cold seemed over, he took his shower early so that he could be in the room with her when she bathed. Over the pages of his *Natural History* he watched her peel the mauve-colored thermal underwear from her dark, glowing body and fill the tin washbasin with hot water from the copper kettle, which was almost the exact color of her face. He watched her soap her cloth and begin industriously if somewhat bemusedly washing her face, neck and ears. He watched her soap and palpate her breasts, and he longed to be where the soap was, covering her deep brown nipples with his tongue. She looked over at him as she moved down her body with the soapy cloth and finally squatted over the pan. John riveted his eyes, which he felt were practically steaming, on a story in his magazine about the upside down eating habits of flamingoes. By the time he looked up she was sitting decorously in a kitchen chair, her feet soaking in the pan. And while she sat, she was busily rubbing something into her skin.

'What's that?' asked John.

The sad truth is that Orelia considered lying to him. And a lot of memories and unpleasant possibilities went through her mind in a flash. She remembered being a little black girl with little skinny, knock-kneed ashy legs, and how every morning her mother had reminded her to rub them with Vaseline. Vaseline was cheap and very effective. Unfortunately Orelia almost always put on too much or forgot to wipe off the excess and so everything she wore and everything on which she sat retained a slight film of grease. This greasiness about herself and her playmates (most as ashy as she) eventually sickened her, especially when television and movies made it clear that oiliness of any sort automatically put one beyond the social pale. The best white people were never oily, for instance, and she knew they put down readily any poor whites and black people who were. So Orelia graduated to Pond's and Jergens, which did the job against her ashiness, but not nearly as well or as inexpensively as simple Vaseline.

She thought about men's need to have sweet-smelling

women, too, while she waited to answer John. Of John's enjoyment of her body when it was perfumed, especially. Actually, as she thought about it, either of them was likely to come to bed in a cloud of Chanel.

Then she gazed into his eyes, veritable pools of trust. Whatever else John expected of her, he never expected her to lie. He expected the best. Fuck it, she thought.

'You got your smell back?' she asked, as she dried her feet.

'Yeah,' said John.

'Well, come here then.'

John came toward her, appreciating her glistening body with its full breasts that had nursed children and now gently sloped, and then stood in front of her. She raised herself against him.

'Smell,' she said. If he fails me it will be just as I expect, she said to herself, waiting for Raymond's betrayal to be duplicated by John.

John sniffed her cheek and neck and rubbed his nose longingly against her shoulder. '*Um*,' he said, somewhat fervently.

She held up the bottle. 'It's olive oil.'

'Olive oil, eh?' he said, peering at the bottle and scanning its fine print. 'From Italy. It sure looks great on you.'

'What do you think of the smell?' she pressed.

'Earthy. Like sandalwood without the sweetness. I like it.'

'You do?' She was suddenly radiant. Her love of John flooding her heart.

He looked at her, puzzled. He never knew what was going to make her happy. Sometimes he felt he just blundered along by the grace of God and hit the jackpot.

'I can cure your dandruff problem,' she said briskly, picking up a comb. 'Sit here between my knees.'

'Which a way you wants me to turn my face?' said John slyly, sticking out his lips and grazing her belly button as he kneeled to put a pillow on the floor in front of her chair.

Orelia carefully covered John's shoulders with a towel and soon she was scratching huge flakes (embarrassingly many and large, to John) off his scalp and explaining how dandruff, especially among black people, was caused not only by a lack of moisture, but a lack of oil. 'We're dryer than most people,' she said, 'at least in America we are. Maybe in Africa our diet takes care of the problem.' She advised that he throw his Tegrin and Head and Shoulders away.

As careful as a surgeon she divided his hair into dozens of segments and poured small amounts of oil between them. Then, using her fingers and especially her thumbs, she massaged his scalp vigorously, humming a little tune as she did so.

After she'd thoroughly oiled and massaged his scalp (which for the first time in months did not itch) she amused herself by making tiny corkscrew curls, 'baby dreads,' she called them, all over his head. She explained that tomorrow he could wash out any excess (though surprisingly the oil seemed to have soaked in instantly and there didn't seem to be any) leaving his scalp comfortable and his hair shiny but without any resemblance to the currently fashionable Jheri curl, which relied solely on harsh straightening chemicals and grease and which they both thought made black people look degraded. 'Hyena-like,' as Orelia described it.

It was all wonderful to John, sitting between Orelia's knees, feeling her hands on his head, listening to her hum and softly talk to him, an intimacy he'd longed for all his life, but one he had assumed would never be for him. His sisters, with their unruly locks, had enjoyed the haven between his mother's knees and between each other's knees, and between his aunts' cushiony knees, as they fiddled with each other's hair, but he, a boy, had been excluded. He imagined himself as a small child and how much he must have wanted to get between somebody's knees; he imagined the first few times being cajoled and then being pushed away. He knew that if he went far enough back in his memories he would come upon his childhood self weeping and uncomprehending over this.

But now. Look.

John knew there was a full moon, he could feel it in

the extra sensitivity of his body, and the fire made a gentle droning sound in the stove; the leaping of the flames threw heat shadows across his face. He felt warm and cozy and accepted into an ancient women's ritual that seemed to work just fine for him too. It turned him on and gave him an idea.

'Let's continue this on yet another plane,' he said.

'Say which?' said Orelia, smiling.

While Orelia sat with hair comb dangling John went and got the futon off the guest room bed and flung it on the floor before the fire; he threw down pillows and covered everything with large towels. Throwing off his robe he entreated her to stretch out on the futon, where he immediately joined her, olive oil bottle in hand.

Soon they were oiling each other like children forgotten among the finger paints. Orelia oiled John's knees and elbows especially well, and as she did so she felt the hurt from Raymond's betrayal disappear from her heart. John, who had long ago learned that we massage the spot on other people that most hurts in us, went to work on Orelia's knees, rubbing a lot but then nibbling and kissing a lot too. Soon they were entwined, the olive oil easing the way to many kinds of smooth and effortless joinings. They laughed to think how like ratatouille and sautéed mushrooms they both tasted, and giggled to be slipping and sliding against each other's bodies like children in mud. And much, much later they fell happily asleep in each other's arms, as oily and contented as any lowlife anywhere. And she was healed of at least one small hurt in her life, and so was he.

Cuddling

(for Tall Moon)

He was preparing a bath for them—she could just hear
him whistling and the water running and imagine
bubbles rising beneath the tap—when she decided she
should tell him. She was sitting on the foot of his double
bed, in which they would soon, after the bath, be lying,
feeling rather sick and starting to cry. What happened
was she would think about Everett off and on all day,
lightly, controllably, but then at night, especially if she
had a glass of wine or a toke, her thoughts tumbled in
upon her consciousness with a weight and abandon that
fairly crushed her. It was that way now.

Sniffling, but squaring her shoulders, she walked into
the bath. John really was gorgeous, with his golden
brown skin and moistly curling hair; she wanted to be in
love with him, not just love him, but could not. That

feeling of breathlessness and joy seemed gone from their relationship. Over the years he had put her through much, including an affair with someone she considered unworth the risk he took to sleep with her, and the elation and trust she had felt for him seemed to die, rather naturally, as a result—not all at once, but bit by bit until the mechanism that tripped the 'being in love' feeling seemed not merely unstuck but uprooted. She had feared it would be absent forever, until she met Everett.

'Such a cheeky, English chauffeur's name,' he had laughed, when they met.

It was. And nothing like him, she thought, at first. Everett was also very attractive, really a beautiful man, with dark brown skin, devilish brown eyes, and a slightly stooping posture adopted to accommodate his great height. Six feet. Not so great, actually, but then she was very short.

John was washing her back when she told him. The rubbing of her back under the shoulder blades as always loosening the tears that in ever greater volume continued to flow.

'It's craziness,' she said, her face hidden from him, feeling the rubbing motion stop. 'But I'm in love—infatuated with—Everett Jordan.

All he said was 'oh.' There was a pause as he resoaped the cloth and then continued washing her—the cloth moving slowly up her back to her neck, up under the ends of her braids. It felt soothing. Maternal. She could never fall in love with a man who couldn't mother her, she thought, sniffling. Now she suddenly felt better. She had told him. It was a problem for them to solve together.

Everett Jordan was a politician of the most effective and cynical type. During election campaigns you could see him beaming at his dozen or so different constituencies over the television, promising jobs, housing, even sexual understanding to those who seemed in need of it among elected officials. In private, however, he was less than sincere. He made fun of people, and hardly seemed to care. But this assessment was made partly to protect herself and was probably terribly unfair. He was more complicated than that, or else, why was she in love with him?

'The point is,' she said to John, facing him and mopping at his chest, 'I don't want to be in love with him. I like our life. He's been married to the same adoring wife for a hundred years. They have fifty-'leven chirrin...and,' she looked into his eyes, 'I love you.'

'But you're not "*in* love" with me?'

'No.'

'But what do you want to do?' he asked her.

'It's impossible. I don't even know how it happened. There we were on the picket line shouting anti-imperialist slogans, and—I don't know—there was, when our eyes kept meeting, as we marched around and around in the snow, a sort of very lively, almost devilish joy, that passed between us. A kind of recognition of all the struggles, all the fallen loved ones, and all the years of being stomped on by crazy people. And all the awful things I'd heard about him—for instance, that he wears eight-hundred-dollar shoes—I felt couldn't, simply couldn't, be true... Of course his boots *did* look like they were made out of some rare creature's skin... And then somehow we slipped away from the march and... had a cup of tea. We were both frozen through. And now we talk a lot on the phone. He keeps me in stitches with his jokes about his jive constituents.' She paused. Laughed. 'See what I mean?'

'And of course there's the adoring wife, the hundred children, and no doubt any number of old dependent dogs.'

His bed always felt wonderful. It did so tonight. It was a little larger than a regular double bed, and he had raised it by placing a kind of platform under it that made it level with the windows that opened over the garden on one side of the room. Under the light quilt and toasty electric blanket she felt comfy and warm.

'I think I might have an affair,' she said. 'If I did, how would you feel?'

'I'd be hurt,' was his prompt, thoughtful reply.

'But I can't have an affair,' she said. 'Too intense. I'm so emotionally involved now that every time I have wine with dinner I start to cry. And he doesn't even suspect anything yet.'

'I wouldn't be too sure of that,' said John, who, as she was speaking, was holding her in the loose, affectionate embrace that had been hers now for a good five years. How pleasant it was, he thought. Its place of importance —holding her, that is—quite unexpected. It was she who had taught him to love to cuddle.

'It's as satisfying to me as "going all the way" is to you,' she'd said. And he hadn't seen how that could be. But then as he blunderingly hurt her again and again and there was the need to make up he'd gotten used to holding her; usually, at first, while she wiped away tears.

She'd cried a lot.

But then, gradually, he came to like cuddling, for its own sake. And then he became a cuddle-addict, and would sometimes surprise her at home, after a horrid meeting or flap at the office, and, virtually limping across the entryway into her apartment, clothes dropping as he loped, 'let's cuddle,' he'd say. And she always would. Sometimes he'd have to wait a few minutes: she might be on the phone. Sometimes as long as half an hour—she might be working or cooking something that could not, just then, be left alone; but soon enough she'd appear in the bedroom door, bright-eyed and enthusiastic, and quite often she would literally leap onto the bed, fling her arms about him, snuggle under his chin, her leg over his, and without further ado they'd lie together blissfully as if in a trance. And he would get up in an hour or so ready once more to face the uncuddly world.

'We must do something,' she said. 'I think I should treat it as an illness. A fever, or something; try to live with it until it breaks. And maybe later,' she said hopefully, 'I can just keep Everett as a friend.'

He suddenly felt very sad for her. This way of dealing with so powerful an attraction would never have occurred to him. Not in the bad old days of hurting her all the time, especially. Then, he'd been so glad he was a man, and could make the first inquiry, the first move. The women had waited for him to do so, he thought, like little rabbits. Not one of them, pursued hard enough, had said no.

Except for her. But then even she had given in and he had thought her no different, eventually, than the rest.

'But I'm *not* any different!' she'd said once when they were discussing his infidelities. 'You hurt us all, but this clumsiness isn't entirely your fault.'

He knew some variation of her women's condition lecture was coming next, and waited for it.

'Women are trained by society not to go after a man they might want, but to wait for him to want them. That's why there's such a demand for new and better, more sweet-smelling and powerful perfumes. Women have been brainwashed to think they're like flowers and have no feet, and that men are bees. Waiting stationary like that makes them anxious. When a man flies by they grab at him eagerly. He's thrown off balance by the sheer awkwardness of it.'

'Is that why women always want you to do something for them, then,' he said. 'Fetch this, carry that. Because they've lost the use of their feet?' He really loathed this about women. The way they made you pay for your pleasures by pressing you into service. If they couldn't talk you into staying around they could at least send you to the store. And how many errands he had run! It made him tired just to think of it.

'Well,' she said, thoughtfully, 'after dark you men are the only ones fairly safe on the streets.'

But now she was in love with someone else.

'Why are you telling me?' he asked.

'I tell you everything,' she said, turning over, curving her back along his body, positioning herself for sleep.

It was the first sound sleep she'd had in weeks. Since the demonstration at which she'd met Everett. Unfortunately she dreamed she and Everett were together in a white antique convertible that kept breaking down when it came to dark stretches of road and along these dark, hidden stretches he kissed her enough to melt the car.

*

She did not get better. The 'fever' did not break. Partly this was because Everett continued to call her very often. His jolly, irreverent voice on the phone the most exciting event of her day. She amused him. A woman's point of view of society, boldly expressed, was every bit as hilarious to him as a homosexual's. She educated him, furthermore (and humorously, of course) about the fastest-growing group of his constituents. Women. Usually single. Usually poor. Usually of color. Usually with kids, and no male influence around. But not always.

Once, for instance, he'd been extolling the virtues of a 'good woman' he knew (later she was to teach him how 'good woman' meant different things entirely to women and men), who he described as long-suffering, hard-working, quiet-spoken, loyal and submissive, but above all, *devoted*, and before he could add that this good woman was his wife, she'd murmured 'Sheepdog.' After he'd finished nervously laughing he'd identified the woman as a distant cousin, blah-blah-blah, who had once been one of his crack campaign organizers. Needless to say, this exchange gave him food for thought that night as he shared a rushed and boring dinner with his wife.

I am free, she thought. Her name, by the way, was Orelia. I have my work—she was a clothing consultant and designer, and extremely good at it—my apartment, a car, grown children, my figure, and my health. And I am in a pleasant relationship with a loving companion who frequently understands me. Being in love is not free. I will stop it at once.

She couldn't.

'I don't even know why I like him,' she wailed to John one evening over a gloomy dinner. 'He doesn't know half the things about women I've taught you. God! To think of going over all *that* ground again.' It would exhaust her final reserves of energy and kill her dead as a nit, she just knew.

She made him laugh, but he could see she was worrying herself sick. She hadn't lost weight—if anything she was eating more, less selectively—and her skin was breaking out. She also was not centered in the least. Nor graceful. Nor—looking at her old denim jacket and gardening jeans—very well groomed.

She thought she didn't trust John. Because he'd had affairs and only told her when he thought (mistakenly, as it turned out) she'd find out. But John felt strongly that on some level she did. He was grateful she confided in him, although it made him suffer—he thought it must always make you suffer when someone you loved was in love with someone else—because it meant they could suffer together, and when the 'fever' broke and Orelia was well they could look back on her 'illness' as one more adventure they'd shared. And they'd shared many.

By Christmas, three months after she'd told him, she

was a wreck. Crying. Biting her nails. Losing sleep. He came across lists on her desk with headings of: 'Good Points.' 'Bad Points.' In the 'Good Points' list, she had written: 'Makes me laugh (though sometimes uneasily). Dresses beautifully. Incredible energy.' On the much longer 'Bad Points' list were: 'Calls women ladies and kisses them automatically instead of shaking hands. Thinks having babies is easy and something all "real" women look forward to. Thinks women vote for him because he "charms" them. Thinks his wife's adoring look is caused by adoration instead of astigmatism . . . ugh.' There was little sparkle in her own eyes and none in her voice.

So John took her away to an island off the coast of Baja, a sanctuary he'd discovered when he'd needed to reknit his own soul after years as a journalist covering the criminal Vietnam–American war. And there in an inn on a cliff overlooking the clear blue water, unreachable by phone, he tended her as carefully as though it were her back that was breaking instead of her heart. Because he understood very well what was making her sick. For the first time in her life she had fallen in love at the same time that she had the experience necessary to know it would never work out. The fighter in her hated the necessity of giving up without a trial, and the lover in her feared imminent death.

Most of their days on the island were sunny and hot. They rose late in their airy suite with its ceiling fan revolving lazily overhead and were brought breakfast on the terrace. Fresh fruit and juice, toast, eggs and the local cheese. For days she gazed wearily out to sea. (She was wondering how they laid undersea telephone lines and how and whether they worked.) It was five days before she commented on the freshly cut flowers that appeared each day, magically, in their rooms. Seven before she admitted enjoying her swims, or drives and walks with John. They cuddled incessantly, as if they were both ill—and in effect they were—and when, in the second week, they began to make love again it was with the gentleness and tenderness and passion that made her smile during lovemaking the way she used to: her merry eyes closed, teeth just showing, skin glowing with delight, so that she reminded him of the little sun face one of his children had liked to draw when he was happy. By the third week she was nearly keeping up with him playing tennis, and her skin had cleared.

He continued to cuddle her, feed her interesting fruits and nuts from the market, order special treats from the kitchen, choose the colors of the daily cut flowers himself, and make love to her as if their lives depended on it. Because of course their life together might. Cuddling for long hours on their bed, seeing the waves of the ocean cresting from their open French doors, Everett Jordan—his look, his voice, his ignorance, his way of making her smile and groan, everything that had so entangled her feelings—faded. She began to see John again. His kindness and sensitivity. His stability and intelligence. His innate gentleness. She felt as if she'd been away from him on a very long, very bad and unnecessary vacation, and easily falling back in love with him on their remote island she wondered how and why. He was wonderful!

She felt like this all the way home. Even as she bounded up the stairs to her apartment, riffling frantically through her purse for her keys because through the door she could hear the phone, ringing and ringing.

Charms

There were days when John thought perhaps Orelia did not love him at all anymore. Sometimes when he kissed her and said 'I love you,' she said nothing, or mumbled 'I love you, too,' as if it were another language, foreign to her mouth. She said it, but he didn't feel it. But this morning, for no reason he could think of, except she had slept well and it was a bright, optimistic day when they woke up, she turned to him, smiled, looked at him carefully, and said 'You're beautiful! And I love you.' John had taken her into his arms and buried his nose in her neck. 'Do you? Do you really?' he'd asked. And she had laughed, squeezed him, and leapt out of bed to do her exercises and spray water on the plants.

Now, as he tinkered with the washing machine, which

was leaking, he thought of how much he had missed her when she went away two years before. She had accepted, for six months, a consulting job halfway across the country; the time had seemed endless to John. He had spent a lot of time in her apartment in the city, sitting in her bed and feeling like crying. Sometimes, watching TV from her big wooden bed, quilts pulled up to his chin, he'd fantasized her cheerful (or glum, it wouldn't matter) face, poking into the room, and felt the vibration of her voice in the air. Several times a week he came simply to be in her apartment, to smell its faint scent of her, to see the stacks of letters that arrived regularly from her friends. Seeing her name: Orelia Moonsun, soothed him. Of course they talked on the phone, nearly every night, but it wasn't the same as seeing her, holding her, and hearing her sensuous or mischievous laugh in his ear.

The washing machine needed a part; he'd found the problem and now held it, a rusting valve, in his hand. He called to ask Orelia if she'd like to go into town with him to fetch it, but she was at the kitchen table busy with some drawings.

Spread out all around her were sketches of a house showing different angles, with lots of cutaways, so you could see where a new room, window or greenhouse could be joined. This particular house was an old Berkeley brown shingle in the flats, and the owner wanted to add a space off the second floor that would permit something of a view.

'It will be strictly an illusion,' Orelia said when she first showed the sketches to John. 'But a nice one. His view will actually be of a long row of his neighbors' backyards, but the addition will be from the one angle that will make them seem to be an uninterrupted garden.'

Finding these special angles for her clients was a great satisfaction to her, and also to those who sought her services—more and more as time went on—for when you entered an Orelia Moonsun redesigned house, no matter where you were, you had the instant illusion of being someplace better. Someplace greener, more spacious, more airy and free.

She herself could never live, really live, in the city, but for those who could or must, hers was the eye to show them how it might be done. She could create a forest out of one tree, a mountain out of a hill, and a meadow out of a handful of flowers and a bush. It was because she needed to leave the city and find a place in the country that she'd gone off on the consulting job. She hated to travel, but the amount of money offered was just enough to make a down payment on some land they'd seen that supported a small house. It had been hard for her to leave him, John remembered, as he drove off to the hardware store; they had both cried.

They'd cried only partly because they would miss each other: they cried because it was so good between them finally: good friends, good sex, good companionship, even good food (they were cooking more together and going out less); they felt the risk the long separation might mean. But she had gone off, because she felt she had to, by train—she refused quite utterly to fly except when she had to cross the ocean—and he had waved after her as the bright blue-and-white Amtrak train left the station.

Then he had returned to her apartment, to her bed, where he had been so happy, where so many discoveries of various kinds had been made, and he had thought, as he often did, of the rather curious way they had met. She'd had cramps. She'd said she had cramps. Anyway, it was the lifetime ago when he was a hostile pre-law student at Columbia (hostile because the very books he must read oppressed his spirit, they were so dully exacting) and he was sitting on a bench in the sun. Orelia had come reeling down the walk, wearing a heavy gray coat, vaguely Russian, buttoned to the chin; the color, herself, of ashes. She fell onto the bench.

There were few black students at Columbia, and none, he had thought, as beautiful as she, but she carried the books, wore the jeans, the leather Frye boots, that were the insignia of Columbiana. On closer look he noticed she was perspiring and that her hands were trembling.

'You okay?' he'd asked.

And with a directness that would never cease to amaze him, no matter how long he knew her, she said, 'I have cramps, and I'm starving to death.'

'Why,' he'd said, 'that's great news; the cramps, I mean.' It was every month to the girls he dated.

She looked at him as if he were a fool.

'It isn't great news?'

She said nothing. Her head had slumped into his side.

By the time she came to, John and one of his classmates had lugged her upstairs to John's room and she was stretched out on the sofa.

'Where am I?' she asked, wryly.

'My room.'

'Won't they kick you out if you have a girl in your room?'

'Not if she's my sister, and not if she's starving.'

He held a bowl of Campbell's chicken soup under her nose.

To which she said 'oh.' When she'd drunk it down she burped, like an infant, and fell sound asleep.

It was an odd feeling, having Orelia there. Several times during the night he woke just to look at her. She'd put on one of his undershirts and his bathrobe, and her short, bushy hair surrounded her thin face like a cushion. He'd heard there were women who starved themselves for the sake of being thin but she was the first one he'd met. The next morning, when he woke up, she was gone. He didn't see her again until the last week of school. By then she was rail thin, and there was a cool, distant glint in her eye.

And then a couple of years later they were surprised to find each other again in a youth hostel in Brussels. She was heading for Paris, he for Berlin. They'd spent the night together, two young Americans lonely and far from home, and she'd seemed in need of comforting; but distracted, too, her thinness by now rather frightening, and she'd listened complacently, after they'd made love (John incredulous that her joints bulged conspicuously in arms and legs) to his announcement of his upcoming marriage.

'I'll never marry,' she'd said with a sigh of relief, as if that were at least one obviously stupid thing she was sure she'd never do.

But then many years later still, he'd heard she'd married. Someone with a profession (John had by then given up law, with the same lightening of spirits with which he was to, subsequently, give up pre-med, psychology and accounting), money, and a big stone house.

Sad to say, shameful to say, too, but though quite often happy in his marriage to Leonie—a smooth, upper-middle-class black Vassar woman, and an irresistible Christian, to boot—there were many, many times when, even though he had never seen it, his thoughts and his heart drifted toward the big stone house. But they were poor. He, in particular, was poor; Leonie came from money: there were famous singers and musicians in her family tree; there'd be money for her when her people died. They lived poor, too, on principle. They both taught, both wrote—mainly pamphlets on various social ills—and with the arrival of their children, a girl first, then a boy, their life seemed happy and full. He did not ask why then was he so often in a marijuana and alcohol daze.

But after ten years he found himself, as if after a long sleep (though his life had been crammed with people, ideas, events, as everyone's is) stumbling up the steps of the big stone house.

Orelia, wearing a long black dress and amber beads that glowed in the shadowy entryway, let him in, introduced him briefly to her own three children who were flying by, and led the way into the mahogany wainscoted lower sitting room.

'And how are you?' he'd enthused, looking furtively about for signs of the husband.

'I think I'm okay,' she said, and then, bluntly, offhandedly, 'I'm getting divorced.'

All thought of the bogus survey of salary levels among black Columbia alumni that he was supposed to be conducting fled. All he could think was: I am too poor to offer this woman anything but a casual affair. Which, after a glaringly brief mumble of inquiry and sympathy, he did.

'Atrocious timing,' she'd said, frowning. 'My husband has cancer, the children don't know yet, and I'm terrified.'

And then followed the years of watching her from a distance, joined only by letters, as she struggled to free herself, her children, even her husband. And at last it was done, somehow. The house sold and the money divided, the children prepared for a different lifestyle, her husband once again healthy and prosperous. A new job invented for herself, a new city. With John following her steps almost exactly, but one year behind, so that by the time she was finally free, he was just on the verge of discussing, with Leonie, the possibility of moving out.

To which Leonie had replied that perhaps they needed to pray. And pray they had, for a year. He could never thank her enough for forcing him to do it, since in the intensity of prayer, which for the first time he took seriously: Please God, let me make the right decision, and not destroy my wife and my children. Please God, let me spend a few years at least with Orelia: he faced his drinking and his marijuana addiction squarely, and rooted drugs out of his life. For Leonie, too, the year of prayer had a positive effect. It helped her to let go. (No feminist, she, the very notion of braving life without a husband, no matter how earnestly he petitioned for release, was anathema to her.) As did the money from a trust fund her family had thoughtfully set up for her and the children for just such an occasion of loss. Though John suspected it was not his going away but his death they had been preparing for.

And so, after innumerable fears, false starts and stops, after much, as he liked to say, mocking Goethe, *strum und drang*, he had 'won', as he thought of it, a few years, at least, with this charming creature, Orelia.

How would they live? Where would they? What work would they do?

'I will support myself, and live in my own space. You and your children, my husband and his children, will sometimes be welcome.' This, from Orelia, which settled quite a bit.

John continued to teach, college-level, now. Slightly better paid. Orelia's business was very slow. She was black, a woman, the service she offered only vaguely understood. She named her company 'Genuine Illusions.' They struggled. They ate a lot of what a friend called *le cuisine de pauvres*, the food of the poor: beans, noodles, suspicious-looking cuts of meat. John lived in a garret. But they were happy.

In fact, they became two of those irritating people who begin a remarkably large number of sentences with the words: 'We are blessed...' and 'I love...' Said with big irritating smiles that made friends want to hit them.

Except that friends felt happy around them, too. For one thing, they were totally without guile, and any fight or disagreement they had, they never considered hiding; and their love for each other, so total and so cherishing, made their friends think automatically of protecting them from any possible damage caused by their own injudicious tongues. It was clear that they thought of themselves not as a couple with private problems, but rather as a private twosome with any couple's problems. And those problems, generously shared, always seemed more interesting to them than whether they could endure having their friends know 'the worst' about them.

For instance, when Orelia, while professing love for John, and obviously feeling it too, still managed to become infatuated with a woman she met at a music festival, their friends, some of whom were, in truth, borderline homophobes, were informed of this. Nothing had 'happened'; she'd touched the other woman's face (and breast); she'd been too frightened at the strong attraction she felt to go on. But there it was.

Some of their friends thought John should leave her; they felt Orelia's attraction to another woman invalidated her as a woman, and called John's manhood into question as well. Some thought Orelia was using her relationship with John as a screen behind which to...but this view could not be maintained in the presence of so much kissing and cuddling between the scrutinized pair. In fact, though much concerned and humanly fearful of losing her, John loved Orelia's spontaneous access to her own feelings, and her lack of shame in expressing them. And even as she struggled with her feelings for 'the other woman,' as they both referred to her, she did not withdraw from John. If anything, she depended on him to help her sort it all out.

Then too there had been the times when John fell off the wagon and back into his old habits of marijuana and drink. It did not seem to occur to them that this was anything but possibly a universal problem: that people slipped into drugs and alcohol when life frightened and appalled them. For John's repurification, Orelia and some of their Native American friends had organized a day of prayer and a sweat. It worked.

A short time after it became clear that Orelia was gone, women began to invite John to their homes for dinner. Soon he was seeing a lot of a woman named Belinda, who taught in his department. She was a divorcée with two children, Ansel, four, and Louise, twelve. At first it was simply awkward, and no matter how warmly she welcomed him each visit he felt like an intruder. Belinda and the children lived in a tiny, neat apartment near campus, with walls so thin he could hear every word of the children's prayers when she put them to bed. After she turned off their lights she came in and flopped down beside him on the scruffy sofa, and leaned her elegant dark head on its back. If she were Orelia, he thought, she'd kick off her shoes and put her feet on the coffee table. No. Not on the coffee table; in his lap. But Belinda kept on her pumps.

Their affair had started when John, thinking of Orelia, asked Belinda if she'd like a foot massage.

Looking questioningly at him out of large, tired, startled eyes, she slowly raised one foot and then the other into his lap. Carefully, he eased the pumps off her feet and began automatically, as he did with Orelia, to rotate her toes.

In a short while she had begun to cry.

'No one ever did that before,' she said, wiping her tears and settling into the pleasure. It always amazed John that there could be so many inept, thoughtless lovers in the world, but he did not comment on this now. The heat in her feet seemed dramatically to increase, until his hands were hot and sliding more and more up her very shapely legs. When he reached her knees—a ticklish spot sometimes on Orelia—Belinda raised herself and met him halfway in a kiss.

Oh, shit, he had thought.

Whereas with Orelia he was treated as an important and crucial part of her life—as she muttered over her work, often not looking all that attractive as she did so, and clearly not caring what he thought about that—John was thrilled to find Belinda eager to make him all of hers. She shopped, with his wants foremost in mind. She cooked expressly to please his palate. She dressed in outfits that revealed the luscious curves of her body, and when he showed an interest in lingerie from Victoria's Secret, she ran up an enormous charge for it on her credit cards. In bed she did everything she possibly could to make him happy. They did not talk much, and she did not seem interested in the work she did at school. But they did not need a conversational life, or so he thought.

It wasn't her fault that he could not forget Orelia, and that even after making the most tender and involved love with Belinda, his thoughts returned instantly to the anticipation of her next phone call. She would be eager to tell him about a new book she'd read, a play she'd gone to. She'd want to talk about how, in the city she was now in, she could make a fortune redesigning houses, because all the houses she saw were so dark, so closed in.

'Nobody on the East Coast'—where she was— 'remembers they used to live in trees!' she cried.

'That's because they actually lived in caves,' he'd replied.

To which she'd said, 'Right.' After a long pause.

On weekends he and Belinda took the children to the zoo, to scientific exhibitions, to museums, to the beach.

He imagined how they must appear to the people around them: a happy married couple and their two kids.

Unfortunately, this image was one shared by Belinda herself, and he began to feel her attachment to it the nearer the time approached for Orelia to come home.

Belinda knew Orelia; not well, but they'd met at the occasional (and Orelia muttered, unavoidable) campus affair. She knew Orelia and John had a life together. She even liked Orelia: liked a middle-aged (Orelia was several years older than Belinda, and looked it) woman who'd reorganized her life; left home and husband, arranged a new life for her children, started her own company. But at the same time, she resented her because she had John, with whom, since the night he'd massaged her feet (and to whose extraordinary ability to comfort and soothe her, she was by now addicted) Belinda had fallen in love.

Oh, shit. John was saying to himself more frequently than ever.

Belinda was not a bad woman, he thought, even as she began to express a lot of verbal fault with the absent Orelia. She had heard Orelia was a man-hater. That she browbeat John. She didn't believe a woman who loved a man should leave him behind for six months.

'She couldn't take me with her,' John joked. Then saw the hurt in Belinda's eyes. 'She has dreams of living in the country.' He shrugged. He listened patiently to Belinda's complaints about Orelia, and sometimes even tried to feel self-pitying, as he studied himself from Belinda's point of view. However, he couldn't stop thinking how tired Orelia sounded some evenings when he talked to her on the phone, her clear homesickness almost made him weep. He found himself beginning to regret the intimacy of this new relationship.

Belinda, whose former husband, a judge, never came to see his children, did not support them, or even, apparently, care that they were alive, insisted that John notice her children's growing dependence on his presence.

Oh, *shit*. He moaned, to himself.

'The kids think you are just great!' Belinda said, hopefully.

And John began to feel extremely guilty, even as he continued to take them to baseball games and to the movies and to the ballet.

In the end, two weeks before an exhausted, delighted to be back Orelia returned, he'd done a despicable thing. He'd simply left Belinda and the kids after dinner, as he had for the past five months, waving and smiling and blowing kisses, and never, except in formal settings— school affairs, church—set smiling eyes on them again. He continued to see Belinda every week on campus, and he saw the look in her eyes. One day she stopped him as he was getting into his car: '*Why?*' she asked.

He'd shrugged lamely, feeling like a cad, and said, 'I'm sorry. I just knew I couldn't be what you need.'

'Am I the only woman you've slept with since she's been gone?'

And John answered truthfully, because he hated lying to women, 'No.'

'You shit,' she said, scornfully. Her anger at least making John feel somewhat cleansed.

He thought about what he should tell Orelia, if the subject of his affair with Belinda (and her children, he always added under his breath, because he realized the children had been wooing him as earnestly as she: and why not, they needed a father) ever came up. Eventually he remembered her telling him about a visit from an old lover and how she had gone out with him and his wife, and how much she still liked him but also how much, unfortunately, she had liked the wife.

The thought that she was still attracted to an old lover drove John into a fit of jealousy. But Orelia had only laughed.

'Everybody I've ever loved, John, I still love.'

'What does that mean?' he'd asked, pouting.

'I think it means, my love, that you will always be safe.'

But he had, in imagination, invented trysts between Orelia and the old lover. He remembered Orelia had said that one of the things she'd loved about him was the fact that he dared to be daring even though he was poor.

'We'd take long trips in his raggedy car, with just enough money for gas. When we came to tollbooths we ignored them. We drove right through. We'd laugh to hear the bells go off.'

John couldn't believe or imagine it. 'Why didn't the cops ever stop you?' he'd asked.

Orelia frowned as if she'd never wondered this herself, though of course she often had. 'I don't know. They never seemed to be around. The real reason though,' she smiled, remembering, 'is that we were charmed.'

'Charmed.' He wanted her only 'charmed' life to be with him.

And one day, in the country, with Orelia puttering happily in her new home, John intercepted a letter to her from Belinda. First he sat Orelia down and told her what he thought was in the letter, then he gave it to her to read.

He was wrong to have been suspicious. Belinda was simply passing along the phone number of someone who wanted Orelia's services as a designer, but the damage had been done.

'Oops,' said Orelia, as the letter dropped from her hands to the floor, like an egg.

There Was a River

There Was a River

There was a river, and they were sitting beside it. It was the only river Marcella had seen in New Mexico. Actually it looked like a canal, it was so straight, as was the path beside it, as was the wooden bench on which they sat. Wordlessly, as if all three had reached a common realization about straightness and man-made designs, they stood up, walked a few steps to the right of the bench, and sat down carefully in the dry grass, balancing gingerly against the pull of the sloped bank.

'We felt we must talk about things,' said Angel. He was short, pale, and closed in, his mouth tense, as if he anticipated unpleasantness. For a long time now Marcella had felt he lacked radiance. Even now, as she looked at him, she wondered: Did he ever have radiance? Or did I create it for him because his mother named him Angel?

Sally, plump and the luscious darkness of a ripe fig, sat between them, her large eyes filled with pain. She had wept so much already she thought no more tears would come. Yet, as Angel spoke, she felt them start up behind her eyes. Damn, she thought.

Marcella also felt out of control. Here she was on a river bank in the middle of nowhere, between her lover and her best friend, compelled, she thought, to choose between them. There was no doubt in her mind that she loved them both, and that to lose either would be devastating.

It had all started because Sally had had a dream in which she'd replaced Marcella in Angel's arms. Marcella had simply disappeared.

'But where did I go?' Marcella had asked, as Sally told her, laughing, about the dream.

Sally didn't know where she went. If she did she never told Marcella.

One evening when the three of them were together in Marcella's house, with its green shutters and wine-colored walls, Sally acted out the dream, flinging herself in Angel's arms and lying back as she'd seen Marcella do. It had been painful to watch, amazingly so.

Now Marcella struggled to articulate a feeling that seemed ridiculous, even to her.

'When you didn't know what happened to me, I felt abandoned.'

'But it was only a dream,' said Sally, pleased that her tears had decided not to flow. Partly, she knew, because her emotions had changed. Angel, as usual, having introduced the agenda, left the two of them to pursue it; suddenly he appeared so vacant it was almost as if he were merely a form. A male form without substance, sitting between them. She wanted to smack him, and say something deeply vulgar and cruel.

Angel was in fact wishing he were someplace, anyplace, else. Marcella, whom he knew so well, was clearly suffering. Her eyes were sad and her voice shook. He felt how awkward his position was: a straw man, a hollow man, between two flesh and blood women. Why could he not feel himself, as he was at least capable of feeling for them?

'I thought you wanted to hurt me,' said Marcella; bravely, Angel thought, considering how she liked to act as if nothing ever could. 'I also thought you . . . '

There was a pause, as Angel read her mind. The word she chose not to say was 'cowardly.'

'I also thought you didn't want to be responsible for it.'

'For what?' asked Sally, screwing up her face, on which the sun shone brightly, causing tiny purple shadows beneath her ears.

'For hurting me.'

'I don't understand.'

'We are not responsible for what we dream,' said Marcella. Wearily.

Angel, from a distance, thought along with her. Yes, he mused. If you tell someone, Hey man, I dreamed about you last night and crushed your nuts with a hammer, what can they say? It was your nightmare. And yet.

'It wasn't so much what happened in the dream, as out of it.'

'Come again,' said Sally.

'That you didn't care what happened to me in the dream I could understand, but when I asked you what happened to me, in your imagination, while I was cooking food for you in my kitchen later, you couldn't even invent something. I disappeared. Okay. I accept that. But what happened to me, in your mind, after you were awake?'

Sally sighed. She really hadn't wanted to tell Marcella, who was, after all, her best friend.

'You were hit by a car,' she said. 'A white Peugeot, moving very fast.'

Five Years Later

Marcella had cooked Sally's favorite dinner, Senegalese chicken and new potatoes in peanut sauce, and Sally had done justice to it by eating every bite on her plate. They sat by the fire after dinner listening to a new CD by a singer Marcella had heard recently in London. Just as she'd anticipated, Sally loved it. Sally had brought her seventeen-month-old grandson, and the two women took turns dancing about the room with him and smiling into his bemused, easily distractable face. During one of these dances, as Marcella swooped and swung and dipped the child to the passionate beat of the music, the phone rang.

Angel, his voice very happy and his speech quite fast, announced he was returning the call Marcella had made the night before, when she called to say good night (just because the moon was full and this had reminded her of Angel and how his fangs seemed to grow on such nights) and had gotten his answering machine. He hadn't answered the phone he said because he'd been 'with someone.' He sounded so pleased with himself, and full, Marcella could practically feel his radiance over the phone. It struck a chord in her; she had a feeling of relief.

They talked, easily, over the phone, Angel describing the color of skin of his new lover—beige, like his own—and quality of hair—curly, like his own—to Marcella, and Marcella describing her evening with Sally and little Basho to him. She mentioned the glowing fire, the crisp cold night outside, the brightness of the moon, the satisfaction she felt sitting and talking and eating with Sally and dancing with the child, who had Sally's dark and soulful eyes and lustrous dark brown skin. She told Angel how 'in himself' he sounded and advised him to do more of whatever it was he was doing. Obviously his one night with the new love had begun to bring him back to himself.

'Don't forget the years of therapy!' he joked, reminding her that for much of his life he'd felt unlovable. The
only time he'd felt loved as a child was when his mother
approved of his performance in school. He'd been a
brilliant scholar, for her sake; left to himself he felt he
would have been happily mediocre. He'd confused love
with approval and felt condemned to perform—in every
relationship.

'But I let you be an outlaw, in our relationship!' said
Marcella, laughing. Recalling the tight jeans and black
desperado stetsons she'd urged him to wear if he felt like
it. The shirts open to the navel and his first gold stud
earring.

'Because I knew that's what you wanted.'

'You mean even your outlaw behavior was a
performance?'

'Yes,' he said.

'Well, damn,' said Marcella, feeling some of the wind
of pride leaking from her sails.

She felt Angel slipping away, and with him a number
of years of her life. If someone has performed the entire
time they were with you what, indeed, was the quality of
your life together? Who was she with? Had she been
alone? She'd often felt alone, as if Angel disappeared
behind his eyes or withdrew himself from his own arms
and fingers. His own face and smile.

The years together were not wasted, though, she

thought, hanging up the phone. Her heart had been broken so many times because of his vacantness, his inability to be there, literally, when she needed him. Eventually, of course, it had taught her to rely on fantasies. Fantasies of other lovers who wouldn't disappear, who would be there for her. It was at the end of her ability to create more fantasies into which to hide the impoverished nature of their relationship that she discovered how alone and lonely she felt, and woke up. A year or so after she broke up her friendship with Sally, she broke up with Angel.

It was Sally, she felt, who'd helped her. Sally and the white Peugeot. Sally who'd perhaps been able to see, as she could not, that Angel was actually oblivious to Marcella, careening wildly as he constantly was away from reality, away from himself. That he, pale and foreign, emotionally, to Marcella, had run over her, killing something in her, in his flight. And it was this that Marcella had feared about her friend's dream. That the person in Angel's arms hardly mattered since he himself was not really there. And that by the time of Sally's dream, Marcella herself had already left.

After putting little Basho to bed Marcella and Sally smoked a pipe of ganja someone had left her as a gift and reclined in the jacuzzi. The moon, nearly full but beginning to wane, lit up the valley below them and a fine mist hung in the faraway trees. The two friends marveled that after years of absence they were back in each other's lives. It was a still, perfect night, with the fresh scent of eucalyptus wafting up from a recently planted grove.

Big Sister, Little Sister

Uncle Loaf and Auntie Putt-Putt

*He dragged her to the bed the first time by the hair,
because he had raised her for it; only she didn't know
what 'it' was. She was yelling and screaming and calling
for her mama. He would get her in the bed and he'd
order her around just like he did when she was doing
work in the house: Lay down. Spread. Put your arms
around my waist. Open your mouth. Suck on my tongue.
He was a big hairy white man whose people had come
from Ireland; he weighed about two hundred pounds and
looked just like a hog wearing clothes. And she was still
a child. She would be crying and gagging, and he would
say: Act natural. Act like it's real good. And she would
have to try to do it, or he would beat her. She was part
Seminole stock, and had that thick, bushed-out hair, full
lips and a high, copper-black color, like a kind of plum or*

maybe a peach you sometimes see, but dark, too, and she had eyes that looked like she was waiting for somebody to die. Not sad, but resigned and impatient at the same time. She outlived his ass, of course; she and the mistress buried him together.

The mistress hated him too, but she hated everybody. She was out there in the middle of nowhere with nobody to talk to but slaves and chickens, and then only when she started the conversation. The slaves would stand and look at the ground, and the men slaves knew it was dangerous to let their eyeballs rise up as high as the hem of her long skirt. They didn't like her and she knew it. And she couldn't talk to him because he hadn't married her to talk to her. He just married her. I think it was because the other white men said it was bad for their little community to have him sowing so many wild oats among the black women, and in general just running around crazy drunk and wild. This is where whiskey drinking came into the family, and stupid behavior.

After he died of a rotted liver, the two women got along a bit better because the mistress turned out to really like children. And all these children by Grandmama were handsome. And she would play with them, teach them to read and write—which was against the law, but nobody ever came way out where they were to check on her—and she let them stay in the big house with her. A big white gloomy thing that looked and felt less like a real house

than like some dead house's ghost. Her plan was to steal
the children away from their mama, who wasn't allowed
in the big house and never knew reading and writing. And
never knew how to act outside of her 'place' as a slave.
But the children would steal stuff from the big house and
take it home to their mother, and she had to sneak into the
back door of the house when the mistress wasn't looking,
and put it back. She didn't love those children much,
herself. She'd have died for them, but she just kept looking
at them like they were strangers until they got grown and
then after Freedom they took care of her and she didn't
seem to mind knowing them. But she always kept her
distance from them, too. You had a feeling of her thinking
she'd somehow given birth to snakes.

Every time I look at them, she would say, I hear him
say: Lay down. Spread. Suck on my tongue. I will tell any
woman old enough to know what I say, that I have spent
years of my precious life, gagging.

When my mother was nearly thirty she married my
papa. And they proceeded to have all of us children. But
she had inherited that standoffish quality from her
mother, who thought laying down with a man was worse
than laying under the wheels of a cart. I don't think she
ever would have gone to bed at night if Papa hadn't come
up to her, taken her by the arm, and dragged her off. She
dreaded going to bed and wouldn't go, until forced, though
she'd married Papa of her own free will and seemed to

really care for him in her own, cool, don't touch me right now, way.

—Gossip Herstory, by
Auntie Putt-Putt

As Big Sister came to the close of this tale, Little Sister groaned. Auntie Putt-Putt had had dozens of stories like this one, and, like the Ancient Mariner, she would grab you by the shoulder, sit you down over a mound of peas to be shelled, and force you to hear them. They'd been the bane of Little Sister's childhood; she had felt instinctively that they wounded something in her, and had avoided Auntie Putt-Putt in favor of books and long walks and the tossing of pebbles into streams. But Big Sister had been hooked, a willing captive. As an adult she compulsively reiterated the stories, much as Auntie Putt-Putt had done. It gave her life a quality of moroseness and easily triggered resentment.

They were now sipping brandy before the fire, in the small cabin that existed on the last tiny remnant of land their family still owned on what had at one time, a hundred years before, been a sizable plantation, whose overseers had been, indeed, invariably Irish or Scottish. Or, over time, a mixture of both. The white descendants of these people were still around, and were seen often on the country roads or on the small town's streets. There was never direct eye contact between them and the Irish-

Scottish descendants, mixed with Indian and African, of darker hue. The black people had traditionally been so profoundly oppressed by the brutality of the white ones, that any connection to them, past or present, was stolidly ignored. In fact, sometimes denied. It was a chilly July evening that made Little Sister think of the Southern expression 'It'll be a cold day in July... before such and such will happen.' Obviously no one twenty years ago could imagine a day in July being cold. But this one was. And so she sipped the brandy gratefully. It was from a homemade batch she'd discovered in a large churn on the hearth; a young cousin had followed the recipe given him by one of the uncles or aunts, and had produced excellent results. The brandy was thick with peach threads, but luscious too and sweet. It warmed Little Sister's body all the way through with a peaceful and a mellow flame. She loved being this way, and didn't, personally, think the Old Irish rapist had anything to do with it.

Left alone in the cabin, while Big Sister swayed out the door on her way to visit a neighbor, Little Sister sat reading in a chair beside the fire. Her lover was coming. He had flown across the country to visit his parents in Covington, a town not far away, and was now, even now, on the road, on his way to see her. She was reading *Wide Sargasso Sea* by Jean Rhys. The freakish cold was hanging on and now it was raining as well. She immersed herself as much as she could in Rhys' sun-drenched foliage, her warm decadent gardens, the magic of the Caribbean! But her mind would stray. Several times she thought she heard the car, and jumped up, a hand flying to her hair, only to sit down in equal parts relief and anxiety. He had brought his wife with him to Covington, and the child. She imagined them all, the wife, the child, the mother, the father, relatives and friends, all happily *en famille*, and felt she should not want to see him. How boring to be in love with someone else's wandering husband! she thought. Yet she did want to see him, desperately. She wanted him with her whole self. Body, and, as they say, soul.

And at last it was unmistakably his car (his father's car, actually, dark, stylish) and then his long legs walking across the yard, head ducked against the rain. And then he was inside, and holding her, and she was nearly sobbing with joy and relief.

He had only a couple of hours, and after the briefest period on the sofa before the fire—a fire he praised, being a great builder of fires himself—they climbed into bed, still smoking the last of a shared joint, and lay for several moments listening to the rain. Lying shameless underneath a large picture of her assembled clan: uncles, aunts, grandparents; her mother and father were there. Oh well, she thought. Now you see me in all my truth.

They were always ravenous for each other. An amazing

state of hunger for her who had always relegated sex to a place near the end of her needs—the influence of Auntie Putt-Putt's stories? she sometimes wondered—and they covered with hands and tongues nearly every inch of each other's bodies. The joint taking effect at just the right moment to ease her coming—at which she cried out dramatically to God, then laughed—and in time to hold him to her as he concluded his own quest. And then, in that time she liked best, the time of rest and stroking, and calming down; the time of looking into each other's eyes; the time of snuggling up and falling into blissful sleep, he departed. Rose—after first glancing at his watch, a habit that frequently annoyed her, but which now actually hurt—and drew on his clothes. Kissed her on the forehead. And left. She felt as if she'd been robbed.

But by the time Big Sister returned, and she had napped, she could hardly believe anything had happened. Semen dripped from her, when she stood, but her body did not remember the orgasm. Luckily she had written it down before she slept.

Big Sister said, next morning: If we can find Uncle Loaf's house, I will be happy. She meant: I will be liberated somehow from the sad stories Auntie Putt-Putt used to tell. If I revisit the place where my unconscious was trained to fixate on the dark, I will become well.

Little Sister knew this was quite a big step for Big Sister, and, though lovesick through and through, roused herself.

Their cousin, who was an outlaw of some sort, who always kept a yard filled with confiscated cars, lent them a car for their excursion, a confiscated taxi—with 'Rapid Taxi,' in bold black letters, printed on its sides. In this they rolled off down the recently paved road in the direction they remembered the house to be. Within minutes it seemed they had reached what had been the turn. They had always walked this road, as children. It had been dirt. It had seemed to take them hours to get anywhere. Yet, here was the turn. They got out, and stared in amazement. Twenty years' uninterrupted growth had closed the road with trees: pines and poplars, scrub oak. They had thoughtfully provided themselves with large sticks which they lifted out of the trunk, and set out.

'I remember all the times I ran away from home,' said Big Sister. 'And I would come to Uncle Loaf and Auntie Putt-Putt's house. And Mama would send Roy or Gail after me. And I would hide behind Uncle Loaf's chair, chewing on some of his tobacco!'

Little Sister also recalled the house, but more vaguely. A three- or four-room cabin, made of pine weathered a soft gray, a kitchen separate from the house, in a clearing surrounded by trees. A lovely spot: quiet, clean, green. It was a time and place where litter did not exist. No one would even have known what you meant. What, trash just laying out on the ground? Who could possibly make sense of that? A cat named First had lived there with the old people. Perhaps there'd been a hound. But her mind attached to none of these thoughts, but was partly, always, on her lover. What is he doing now, she thought, at just this moment?

'Always running away to enjoy life,' Big Sister was saying, hitting at a bush with her stick, to scare off, possibly, snakes, 'and always sent for, caught, and brought back.'

'You were adventuresome,' said Little Sister, supportively. But underneath this comment she thought: You always ran to the same place (yet, where else was there to go?) and you always let them find you, catch you, and bring you back.

'Not as adventuresome as you. You got clean away, from the beginning.'

The path was rocky, hilly, branches of trees struck them in the face. They learned quickly to raise their hands and sticks.

'Ah, my adventures are killing me,' she said glumly. But Big Sister did not wish to hear. As far as she was concerned, Little Sister had no serious problems. Though she admitted she looked haggard and tired, as if she had not been sleeping well. Still, she felt an overwhelming need to have what attention there was focused on herself.

Little Sister thought: Love is the hook. I simply did not love them enough to let them hook me. I created a critical distance between us. You could be called upon to cook, to clean house, to care for all the children that came after you, including me. You were deliberately conditioned to put yourself last. They used your love for them to make you comply with their every wish. But I watched what they did to you—and decided not to love them more than myself.

Big Sister thought: It is her selfishness even now that is butting in. 'My adventures are killing me!' Indeed! A gorgeous husband, a gorgeous child, a gorgeous house, a gorgeous career! Even the luxury to be moaning and groaning over a lover! And what have I got? An ex-husband I should have divorced before I married him. Children who neither call nor write. A house so unstable it would blow away if my gimme this, gimme that sisters and brothers' children didn't hold it down by their sorry, no'count weight.

They had now reached an impasse. Over the remains of a barbed-wire fence a thicket of vines, trees and bushes had grown. The vines connected to and extended themselves by covering the large oak tree that, years ago, had fallen across the path. If they went around it they were fearful of losing the faint path they'd discovered. They could not go over it.

They stood, the two sisters, looking about them.

Little Sister realized that finding the house was not important to her. Big Sister herself was. But would Big Sister now say: It is impossible, this effort to go back and be released from the past. Useless. Let's go back, before the rattlesnakes smell us? Her shoulders were slumped. Her face, so happy and confident when they started out, dejected.

Big Sister thought: I cannot go it alone. I cannot lead. This was where she thought the biggest flaw lay in herself. But Little Sister can, has, and will. Big Sister thought this, resentfully. She never ceased to be faintly annoyed by Little Sister's optimism, and felt this way now, even as she waited to hear Little Sister's confident: We can do it, come on! In her imagination Little Sister was leaping the barricade of the fallen tree with a single bound, bullets and rattlesnakes repelled by her Wonder Woman-like bracelets, and with a no-bullshit determination pulling Big Sister along with her, through the air.

'I will sit here,' said Little Sister, as if overhearing this fantasy. Choosing a rocky spot, clear of snake holes, she sat down. 'Until you decide what we should do.' She settled herself, pulled out a piece of gum, offered Big Sister one, and began, herself, to chew. Calmly, into space, like a cow.

Big Sister thought: It's just like her to sit down, to wait, not to help. To know nothing of housework, or cooking; to pretend ignorance of everything that looked like work. Oven cleaning, for example. She doubted if Little Sister even knew there was such a thing, and had certainly never cleaned an oven herself. What struck her was the way Little Sister had seemed, from the beginning, resigned to going it alone. And because it was apparent to everyone that she would go alone, they leapt forward—or so it had seemed to Big Sister—to help or to accompany her. Over the years she had watched her. And what she'd seen was that Little Sister did only what she pleased. What she pleased to do was smoke, drink, pet with boys, who were always hanging around sick with love at the sight of her, study, read long novels, go with their mother on long, mainly silent, walks...to come home hungry for a dinner Big Sister prepared. Her mother instantly lifting the tops off pots, peering into the oven complaining about something. 'I really prefer it more done, myself.' Or: 'Are you sure these greens were washed three times? There's a feel of grit.' And then her father, gulping down everything without a word, as if he didn't taste it, and her brothers, saying the biscuits were lumpy and throwing them at each other like rocks.

And Little Sister. The most irritating of all. Because she alone never complained or criticized. She would eat, daintily, as if from a country foreign to siblings, her well-scrubbed left hand in her lap, her attention completely on the flavors of the food. 'Wonderful!' she'd breathe, as if eating itself was miraculous. And the taste of food cooked by Big Sister, nothing short of sublime. She would smile at Big Sister, and after dinner she would gratefully, carefully, but completely absentmindedly, wash and dry the dishes. Then she would retire to her room to read, or walk to the mailbox and back, or she would sit on the front porch and, apparently, listen to the crickets. The way she did the dishes, automatically, never noticing them, made it seem that she never did housework at all. It was the same with dusting the furniture or sweeping the floor. Twenty years later Big Sister understood that though Little Sister's hands were on the broom she swept with, her mind was on alabaster castles and gremlins and dwarves. On knights and round tables that never knew dust and on swords that, through enchantment, remained stuck in stones. Big Sister never remembered Little Sister doing housework because it was as if Little Sister was never conscious of doing it. It was there, she did it, but it had no place in her consciousness. But most of all, thought Big Sister now, because I was there, Little Sister did not feel responsible for it.

That was the difference. And nobody complained... But wait, they did complain. And what happened? Little Sister would simply put down her book, the broom, the garbage pail, the dish of eggs she'd fried to a crisp, and simply look at the complainers. Being compelled to come back to face them from whatever fascinating place she'd been would have had an obvious impact on her happiness. Who are you, and what are you to me, anyhow? her look said. It unnerved them. They conceded her craziness and left her alone.

The ground on which Little Sister sat was hard. It eventually became uncomfortable. Little Sister watched Big Sister stand there, and look despairingly at the barrier. Did Big Sister really wish to continue? Yes. Little Sister could see that she did. Little Sister rose, pulling herself up by her stick, and followed the thicket-covered fence to the left far enough to see they would become lost in that direction; she then beat her way across to the right, where the thicket grew over the fallen tree. On that side she thought they could wriggle through a sort of hole in the thicket. Big Sister, meanwhile, had this thought herself, but had rejected it. It had something to do with her weight, her size. Could she wriggle through? Would there be 'another side' to come out on?

'Well, I say, let's try it,' said Little Sister. But she was smaller. Not slender, but rather curvy, and had never had a problem with her weight. She could surely wriggle through, Big Sister thought bitterly. With a resentment so strong she acted quickly, against her own belief—which was that she was too fat to make it—to plunge into the leafy 'hole' before her; Little Sister following close behind.

For several minutes they seemed imprisoned in leaves,

branches, briars, tall prickly weeds. If there were snakes they were in for it: trapped, they'd be unable to extricate themselves fast enough to get to a doctor.

Oh, well, Little Sister was thinking: If I die, maybe my lover will notice. Maybe he'll leave his wife. Maybe he won't leave his wife—which seemed more likely—but will grieve to have missed so much excitement by my early death. Still, being bitten by a snake in a thicket in the woods, miles from help, was not the way Little Sister wanted to go. Except, and here she stopped short, struck by a thought, as she watched Big Sister, as Pioneer, hack away at the bushes in front of her as if murdering someone. Except that, even though she thought Big Sister might not be exactly grief-stricken over her death, she would like to have her Big Sister with her when she died. This was not a thought she'd had before, and certainly not one she'd had on this trip. But now she let herself sink into the knowledge that yes, as children, Big Sister had always taken care of her, in sickness and in health. She had especially taken care of all of them in sickness: through measles, flu, broken limbs even. She had made of herself a service and a comfort, with a soothing bedside manner that Little Sister had loved. Big Sister would never be impatient or mean, as Little Sister felt she might be, toward a sick person. But, Little Sister thought, continuing to walk behind the broad back of Big Sister, when I am not sick, she resents me. She is murdering me while attacking those bushes, even now.

'There's light!' said Big Sister, as they emerged once more on the path.

Little Sister hated to think of her lover now because this was obviously an important journey; one that belonged to her and to Big Sister. That was the trouble with 'being in love'—the person in love was a bit deranged, not herself. Distracted, mentally harassed. Miserable and locked inside herself. They now approached an ancient oak thick with mistletoe.

'Uncle Loaf's brother, Tarry, as in Tarry-Along, lived here,' said Big Sister with delighted assurance. 'Uncle Loaf's house is just ahead.'

Little Sister had not known about Uncle Tarry. Why had the brothers lived so close together, she wondered. For protection? Because they owned a small plantation during Reconstruction that shrank around them? Because they liked each other's company so much they enjoyed living practically in each other's yards?

And, good God, what must it have been like, stuck way back here in the woods, off the main dirt road? Little Sister forgot her lover long enough to feel a familiar terror of the past. She could never return to the past and survive. She knew that. To be a nineteenth-century black woman; to be an eighteenth-century one. How had they stood it? To be a slave. A slave, whose every move was planned by someone else. Not to love where you wanted, who you wanted. With this thought her lover's face returned. She moved up beside Big Sister who now stood motionless in a small clearing, facing a mass of vines and bushes, and the collapsed gray remains of what had been the kitchen/laundry of Uncle Loaf and Auntie Putt-Putt's house.

Big Sister's face was radiant. A condition Little Sister had rarely seen. 'I've found it!' she said. To this place she had run to find love and dream and freedom. Here, chewing Uncle Loaf's tobacco, she had been a person of leisure; as Auntie Putt-Putt, always puttering, as everyone said, cooked and cleaned and kept the fields going, or walked to the roadside market five miles away to buy matches, snuff and kerosene.

But they, her parents, had always come after, or sent for her. She had been dragged from behind Uncle Loaf's chair and off the sagging porch. Uncle Loaf only mildly defending her. While she was there they treated her kindly. He gave her sticks of peppermint candy. She handed him earthen cups full of water or sweet wine. Auntie Putt-Putt told her stories. 'Come back,' they'd call, as she was hustled down the path. 'Come back to see us.' And yet Auntie Putt-Putt must have guessed that, though enthralled by her horrible tales, it was Uncle Loaf she really came to see.

But on their invitation, Big Sister always snuck away from the chores at home, and returned. Whippings didn't deter her. Being kept home from school to wash the family's dirty clothes didn't either. In later years she would think about the imbalance of his sitting at his ease, being served like a prince, while Auntie Putt-Putt worked so hard. But she could not have complained, or even noticed, at the time. Because sitting at his ease was how she wanted him. His sitting there, daring to do nothing, was what assured her a sense of freedom, of escape.

Now she saw it. They dragged her home where she became... Auntie Putt-Putt

'Don't go in,' she called to Little Sister, who was poking around the kitchen ruins.

'Don't worry,' she said. 'I thought I might unearth some crockery that you'd recognize.'

Little Sister thought: If I had run off here I would have roamed the woods, hung out in the trees. Nature is notoriously more spacious than front porches. But Big Sister had come to sit and then to hide behind Uncle Loaf's chair, and he had known each time that they would come for her. Never did he say: Don't take her.

They were jubilant with success on the way home, looking at the instant photographs that verified their adventure. They pulled into the curved road that led to the cabin in a squall of giggles and gossip, and of bragging. Little Sister was driving and thinking very little of her lover, except to regret his absence from the fun. At the cabin she suggested a swim, and they threw off their clothes and plunged into the lake wearing only their underwear; Little Sister's a bikini-like set by Lily of France, bronze against her deep brown skin; and Big Sister in a more matronly Maidenform. Black, with a good deal of lace.

Blaze

Little Sister dreamed frequently of her lover's wife. 'I dreamed,' she said to Big Sister, as they lay drying off beside the lake, 'that she, that is, her parents and she, had a maid when she was little. A black woman. I dreamed this woman spanked her, but also cared for her, as black maids do. And that that is why she is longing to reconnect with black women. She misses them.'

'Them?'

'Well, the experience of them that could be embodied in one.'

Little Sister remembered her own childhood and one of her best friends, a white girl named Blaze. Remembered the day her parents brought her to play with Blaze as usual, while her mother cleaned house for Blaze's mother, and Blaze's father had said: 'Miss Blaze isn't here today. She'll be back...' But she never came back for Little Sister or for her parents, who understood perfectly what they were being told: No more equality. No more friendship. 'Miss' Blaze. And Blaze, like Little Sister, was only twelve years old.

For the life of her Little Sister couldn't recall anything she and Blaze had done together. They must have waded in the creek behind the house, caught tadpoles, made baskets out of willow rushes. Climbed trees. Played on the swing. She'd blocked the memories, of course. It was all, the experience of being demoted, turned away, blocked by rage. She had thought Blaze had decided it was time her friend called her 'Miss' Blaze, but now that seemed unlikely. What child could have been perverse enough to think like that? At twelve or thirteen would it have seemed so important? It might. Because there had been white society, such as it was in those parts, to think of. Her white friends would have been her true peers. They would have been at an age to begin to understand it was possible that their mothers bought the friendliness and compliance of the black women who appeared magically at the back door of their invariably white houses each morning.

There was the rage, a shut door that seemed to be made of iron; but then way behind it, in the fields that encompassed her childhood, under a blue sky that was endless and magnificent, was the friendship, right in there with all the other good things of life. A time of mutual trust and happiness. And an unawareness of inequality, only the enjoyment of mutual sweetness. The barely worn dresses Blaze's mother, and Blaze herself, insisted she take for school, and the firewood, walnuts, handmade rocking chairs her parents gave to Blaze's family. But Little Sister refused to remember this emotionally. Refused to permit it any validation in her feelings. Because to do so, she felt, would be to become complicit in her own betrayal. And she felt she had been betrayed. No 'good ole days' could ever exist for her, once she understood that even her happiest days rested on a foundation of inherited evil. An evil that said, when she least expected it: 'Miss' Blaze...

And yet.

Now she began to understand that the dream was about her own longings, not about her lover's wife's. For though she blocked any feelings except rage and contempt for Blaze, of course their friendship, or, rather, relationship, remained unresolved. Unfinished. It was as if they'd been playing an engrossing game of chess and someone unconnected to the game, they had thought, had suddenly snatched away the board. There they sat, startled, unprepared to continue without a structure, on opposite sides of an empty table. Nothing connected them anymore.

She would pretend later that her only girlfriends growing up were black. Blaze, no doubt, had pretended her only friends were white. And they had each gone to bed at night determined to forget and forget and forget. She had never set foot in Blaze's house again, after her father's comment. She wondered if anyone had explained to Blaze what had happened. Now she could imagine the cruelty of it, from Blaze's point of view. To return home, expecting to see the bright face of your friend, someone you loved, and to have that bright face, without explanation, never again appear.

What is not remembered emotionally, Little Sister had thought, is not remembered. But look at her adult friends. They were so often Blaze all over again. And in fact, it was through these white women who were her friends as an adult that she discovered what Blaze was like. She no longer remembered Blaze herself at all, but these women were invariably timid, sweet, docile, confused, morally lazy, loving and generous. They would not stand up for themselves, however, and she would soon feel the rage—because if they could not stand up for themselves, and they at least had the power of whiteness in a white supremacist society—they would certainly never stand up for her, or for real friendship or sisterhood with her. Yet, seeking to complete the 'game' with Blaze, she picked these women again and again. Whereas her black women friends were chosen primarily for their challenging spirits, however envious, competitive, flighty, or, yes, confused and morally lazy they might be. The ones she really adored would stand toe to toe with the devil himself and yell Fuck you so loudly he'd cover up his ears.

Her mother, because she needed to work, was not able to escape 'Miss' Blaze, and called her that, always, even if there were no house guests or other young white people who'd come to call.

'No,' she would say to Blaze who asked her to call her what she'd always called her, 'your daddy says you're a young woman, and young women are called "Miss."' It was a wedge between them. Deliberate and effective.

Was that it? Was that the source of the rage? Not what was attempted against Little Sister, which her mother helped her to escape by not permitting her to return to Blaze's house, but what was forced on her mother, who could not escape? Little Sister had lived out her childhood at a time and in a place that permitted her to see both a remnant of slavery and a possibility of freedom. But the possibility of liberation was the gift she was unable to give her mother, just as the remnant of slavery, 'Miss' Blaze, was the burden her mother refused to pass on to her.

Little Sister was unaware that her thoughts were causing her to glower. Or that she was staring at the surface of the lake as if a monster lurked just beneath. But she heard chuckling, and noticed Big Sister was looking at her.

'Stop frowning, you'll get wrinkles,' she said. She sat on a blanket she'd brought from the backseat of the car, and sat oiling herself in the warmth of the afternoon sun.

'Changes, changes,' said Little Sister, smiling briefly. 'Does anything ever turn out the way you expect it to?'

'I don't think so,' said Big Sister. 'I never even thought it would be warm enough today to swim.'

Little Sister nodded, and returned to her thoughts.

She thought about how hard it was to read the stories she sometimes received at the women's magazine where she worked because in them white women were talking about their closeness to the black women who had nurtured them. Each time she read such a story, she encountered her rage afresh. Embittered by the possibility, the probability, that their black servants *had* nurtured, *had* loved them, as one particularly sincere writer wrote, 'unconditionally.' It was a love compelled by forced circumstances and forced familiarity—similar to the forced affection one felt for certain likable white characters on TV. There they were, every Saturday night: Mary Tyler Moore, Bob Newhart, the *M*A*S*H* contingent; and they were silly and witty and bright. And you cared about them because they were there, and you liked television, and they were the best white folks to watch in a predominantly white medium.

Perhaps she was enraged because she had hoped love between maid and miss was impossible. That was obviously what every little girl whose mother was a maid hoped. For how could you compete with the little girl who had everything, could buy everything, including your mother? And had been buying your mother for centuries.

You could hate your mother for loving someone for whom she had to work. Perhaps. But how could you, since she worked for your benefit, because of you? The pain was because you felt she loved against her will. Because 'If you can't be with the one you love,' as the song went, 'love the one you're with.'

Now she felt the source of the tension she experienced, working at the modestly integrated, white women's magazine. She could not complain about the behavior of the women toward her. They went out of their way, for the most part, to welcome her, to support her, to assure her they recognized her value not only to them, but to the world. And yet, each time she walked into the office she had to seclude herself for several minutes, in order to get hold of her breathing. And she was there by choice. But not totally.

The black woman who cleaned the office at night was there, like her mother, because she, doubtless, had children and herself to feed. She knew that that woman too had difficulty breathing, as surely as her own mother must have had. Or maybe not. Because cleaning an empty office was just a job. Working with the white women every day was somehow more, because you were drawn into relationships with them, and sometimes you genuinely cared. So perhaps the question was: Is not affection or love something pitiful, and degraded, when it is compelled by circumstances beyond your control? And when to choose not to love, or to feel affection, represents a greater danger to the soul than one's simple inability to do so?

She watched Big Sister floating on her back in the water, the oil she had slathered on earlier making a greasy circle around her. She thought of her lover, of their trips into the country. The way they would pick an especially hot day to go exploring the countryside, and then swim in every lake, in every park, they came to. How they would lie on the grass, smoking grass. How she liked to sing with him. How he sang. And yet, no matter how happy they were, there was his wife, and the child, and Little Sister's obligatory worrying about them all. She was beginning to wonder how anyone ever had the strength to have affairs.

Lying on her back, watching the sun begin to sink behind the pines that ringed the lake, Big Sister began to feel like someone other than, different from, her usual oppressed self. She found herself immersed in a memory whose energy seemed about to suck her out, permanently, from her former life of gloom. This felt very strange. And yet, and this occurred to her for the first time: Something odd like this always happens to me when I spend time with Little Sister! She was remembering the day that she had had a different experience, from all the earlier ones, of Uncle Loaf and Auntie Putt-Putt.

She was eighteen, a young woman, and about to go off to school, several small towns over, to learn to be a veterinarian. She was dressed in a green plaid jumper, a crisp white blouse with a pointed collar, and her first pair of high-heel patent-leather slippers, which she wore with stylish Red Fox stockings. Her hair was waved away from her face and reached a kind of crest on top. She wore gold earrings and a necklace she'd received from her current boyfriend. The one she would have married if she'd had sense. She had liberally anointed herself with a cheap, bright-smelling perfume.

For years they had not really said much beyond 'Howdy,' or 'How you?' To which the answer was, invariably, 'Oh, tolerable. You?' They did not go beyond these preliminaries now. Big Sister settled herself, not behind Uncle Loaf's chair, as she'd done as a child, but beside him, in a chair identical to his own. He sat as usual, leaning backward against the wall in a wooden chair near the water shelf, which Big Sister noticed had recently been repaired. The last time she had visited, the nails had been coming loose, and the shelf, under its gallon bucket of water, sagged. She noticed that the railing of the porch had also been straightened where it bulged near the steps, and the steps themselves strengthened.

Auntie Putt-Putt came out of the kitchen, crossed the porch in front of them carrying a basket. She wore a large round straw hat, a faded yellow print dress made from feed sacks, and an ancient pair of sneakers without backs, so that her heels looked hard and gray as she walked down the steps and toward the garden.

Then, and Big Sister could not believe her eyes, Uncle Loaf brought his chair down onto the porch floor with a plop, went into his private room, the 'front room,' and returned wearing his own large straw hat, washed thin and very faded khaki shorts (for he had fought in World War I and returned home 'shell-shocked,' a word that everyone in the family used in discussing or describing him, but the meaning of which no one knew) and a soft white cotton shirt. On his arm he also carried a basket made of white oak strips, with a broad curved handle the color of his deep brown skin. He moved quietly and calmly down the steps toward the garden and his wife, Big Sister following, on her toes, protecting her shoes against the scraping rocks, wood chips and chicken doo-doo. Surprised. Flabbergasted. Wondering. Unbelieving.

What was this? It was as if the quiet oak tree in the yard had suddenly shaken itself and begun to meander down the road.

Big Sister stood in the shade of the corncrib's overhang, watching. Auntie Putt-Putt did not seem to notice anything different. Nor did Uncle Loaf. Their goal was to collect the tomatoes that she sold to the local store, where they got their kerosene. Uncle Loaf started on a row next to Auntie Putt-Putt's but coming from the opposite direction. So that, as Big Sister watched in wonderment, forgotten by these two old people in their green universe hidden from the world, they met, but still did not acknowledge each other's presence, or the fact that a miracle had occurred. They stood a moment, swaying their backs against their hands, shifted their baskets, and continued serenely along their separate rows.

When Big Sister was leaving them, they sent tomatoes to her family. Still Uncle Loaf said nothing, and, for once, Auntie Putt-Putt seemed out of ancient family gossip. Uncle Loaf went to his room and returned with a handful of silver dollars. He handed them to Big Sister. 'Far away,' he said. They did not kiss her. They had never kissed her. They were people of the hug. Their hug, reserved, as they were, was the circle of the world known so far, the rounded silence of their hidden universe. And she had walked out of their embrace, free at last.

Recalling this day now, as she lay once again beside

Little Sister, who had fallen asleep, Big Sister began to feel health, balance of spirit and soul return to her. She saw that she too had been seen as someone deserving of getting away. Not Little Sister alone. She too had been supported. Not just frightened and burdened down with other people's children and horrible tales of woe. She too had been helped.

As she thought of this, and turned to Little Sister to tell her how that last day of her childhood had been, she noticed that though usually so cheery and confident, she had started, in her sleep, to weep.

'Ah, wake up, Little Sister, it's not as bad as all that!' Big Sister said gently, shaking her.

And true to her irritating self, Little Sister, tears still rolling off the side of her chin, opened her eyes and endeavored to smile.

'Oh, cut it out,' said Big Sister. 'I see those tears!'

'You do?' said Little Sister, surprised.

'Yes!' said Big Sister emphatically.

More tears appeared instantly in Little Sister's eyes. She began to sob, much as she had when she was a child. She cried, leaning against Big Sister's shoulder, until there were no tears left. And sure enough, soon she was smiling for real, because she was with her Big Sister, after all, and they were celebrating the close of a very happy day.

Growing Out

Growing Out

And then there was the night Anne realized she had outgrown the woman she was. It was Jason's birthday, and he had brought a bag of magic mushrooms.

How much do you weigh? he asked. One hundred and thirty pounds? Well then, you should have—this much. And he put several stems and a cap into an earthern dish. Magic mushrooms! She thought of Aldous Huxley, who had eaten them, and of Carlos Castaneda, who must have eaten *lots* of them. She thought, for some reason, of Julius Lester. Perhaps because he used to read Huxley over WBAI radio when she still lived in New York, and she had gone out and bought *lots* of Huxley, and had been bored. She never found the fascinating insights in Huxley's work that Lester had. Well, maybe Huxley's words had sounded profound in Lester's voice? A deep, black-rich voice. Not at all like Jason's. Jason's voice was light, almost high. When he deepened it deliberately, while striking a mock superblackman pose, they both laughed, it was so absurd. There was in it a tentativeness, a gentleness, that moved her. So she cooked the lamb chops she had prepared (vegetarianism not yet having entered her life) while nibbling on the mushrooms. Alive to the vibes and smells in her kitchen, and to the sunset that was reflected off the trees near the patio.

He loved the light as the sun was setting. The angle of the sun to the earth was changed. No longer perpendicular, or even on a slant. But seeming to shine upward, from beneath the earth, somehow. And it was limpid and golden. And she felt, with the music of Spanish guitars coming now from the adjoining living room, a kind of thankfulness that she felt more and more strongly these days—now that she had recognized God in Nature, and had given in to love, and she was happy, happy! And so she chewed all of the magic mushrooms—surprised how like mushrooms they tasted, and she turned frequently, for no reason except that she loved him utterly, to embrace him.

They were alone. The children at: goat farm, other parent, on overnight with friends. And it was a good thing.

First they ate. Then she sang happy birthday to Jason

as he smiled and blushed. Rising from the small wooden table, and clearing her throat theatrically, she also presented him with a poem. Her first 'occasional' poem that spoke of their life together. Its struggles. Its adventuresome times, both high and low. The lamb had been tender and delicious, the broccoli crisp. The wine that followed, a Simi chablis they'd bought directly from the winery on one of their country visits, chilled and perky. After dinner, they felt they might dare to watch a TV special on the Old Apollo up in Harlem. How it had been in its heyday. She saw again how black people had looked to her in the Fifties: sweet and hopeful and bright, in clothes and hair that made you laugh. She remembered them that way: innocent.

A few of the stars were even then on the drugs that would eventually kill them. But not the ones she loved. Well, Frankie Lymon ('Why do birds sing so gay, and lovers await the break of day, why do they fall in love... Why do fools fall in love?') was almost the only one to OD on heroin, she thought, but there were probably others. She had been in high school in Georgia when the young singer died; like all her female classmates, she had idolized Lymon (who must have been all of fifteen years old) and had endlessly fantasized about him.

Settling back against Jason's warmth on the cushy sofa, across from the TV, she now saw how the show tried to exalt the man (in the person of Lou Rawls) higher than the two main women singers, Gladys Knight and Natalie Cole. And how he seemed to be singing from his throat only, while looking off seductively into space, and how the women, very graciously, attempted to be less, but could not quite manage it. No matter how low they sat, or how much the script called for them to look up to him, or how calmly they tolerated his vacant 'seductive' gaze that just grazed their vivid faces, they could not make themselves less powerful or smaller than he was. Gladys Knight was actually funny trying to hide herself, her talent, her force. Finally, she and Natalie Cole (who seemed ashamed of her black, Fifties-looking father, with his thoroughly conquered hair, and showed only the briefest glimpses of him on old film clips) stole the show away from him. And did it without ever rising, physically, to his level. They were 'ladies,' after all, and so the script required them to remain seated the whole time. So that their triumph, gracious to the end, was that much more amazing.

Anne began to laugh, and then to cry, at his emptiness (a voice in a human box, she thought), so apparent on the screen. And then Ben Vereen, who always seemed to be Tomming to her, came on, acting the role of black genius forced to deal with arrogant Jewish impressario, and she forgave him for wanting to dance so much that he appeared to suffer, willingly, the condescension of white patrons. Because of course he was probably no more willing than Bert Williams, a half century before him, had been, or any of the other early singers and dancers. She recalled his role as 'Chicken George' in *Roots* as being self-loving, but was he in fact self-loving in real life? That he might be mattered to her. Then Flip Wilson came on in blackface—with Nipsy Russell. Both so outrageous. She finally understood something about blackface. That it could be funny. But not the way white people had done it, to make fun of blacks. It was funny only when it made fun of human gullibility, human frailty and craziness—as blacks had used it among themselves. On closer look, she saw that Flip had somehow managed to put on a black face over a white face which was over his own brown face. Blue eyes looked out, stupid and immense.

She cried, looking at the men who now stepped up to the microphone: the Mighty Clouds of Joy. So much expansiveness, so much lightness, expressed in the name they gave themselves, she thought. Every one of them so heavy, too. They would all have been so perfectly at home with a dish of pork chops, greens, candied yams. So at home, also, with the spirit they sang to and for. They were real, earthy, generous-hearted, scarred and puffy-eyed, singing for Jesus. And she loved them because they remained who they were through it all.

The tears would well up, sometimes just as she was laughing. For instance, it amused her that Natalie Cole might consider herself less funny looking than her father. And not just Natalie Cole, but, it seemed to Anne, that this was a common delusion of black people, or maybe of people in general; that we look less funny than our parents. However, with our high unemployment, our high infant mortalities, our uneducated young, or drug-infested youth and adults, our pathetic schools, our laughable national leadership, our oppression by greedy and racist people, we are *just* as funny looking as our parents. We might even be *funnier* looking because there is so much less hope, and it is so much later in the day.

Jason held her, stroked her back, and she felt his strong heartbeat under his cheek. They'd forgotten magic mushrooms had this effect on her: tears and laughter, perfectly mixed. Or perhaps they did not care. She did not. She actually loved tears, once she was in the release of shedding them, because she knew laughter was just beneath them.

After being exhausted by the show, they listened to music. She said: Let's hear some Billie Holiday—and put on a tape. But right away she felt the change: the first song was something about 'When my man quit me, you know I felt so sad.' The next one was about a beating. Her man, beating her. She and Jason exchanged looks. Dismayed. Let's hear something else, quick, he said.

Anne was puzzled. I used to love this music, she cried. Remember how we played it that month in the country?

How I used to play it when we were apart? 'I must have that man.'

Well, said Jason, we loved Lester Young, too, and he still sounds okay. But Billie's bringing me down.

Me, too, she agreed.

Then she knew who would not bring them down because she would not bring herself down: Bessie Smith.

Soon she and Jason were lying comfortably snuggled together, reminding each other in whispers of Bessie's exploits with her male and female lovers: jumping out of windows, being chased out of town, doors broken in, almost being run over by a car. Her husband Jack never quite catching up with her. Laughing, enjoying her spirit, they sang merrily along with her, her rich broad country accent making them snort with glee. They played the songs they particularly liked over and over.

Jason ruffled her short, curly hair.

It's butch, he said, but I like it.

It is? You do?

Anne ran to look at her face in the mirror. Yes. She saw what he meant. She went to the full-length wall mirror. There she was: blue jeans, silk blouse open to her breasts, barefoot and short-haired. Butch.

She ran back into the living room, took him in her arms, and laid her tongue deep in his mouth.

She had told him that she had loved and still loved a woman. But that she loved him more, and so she was with him. Perhaps a day will come when you love her more, he said. Perhaps so, she thought. But could she really be happy with someone named Jerri?

Why is it that so many lesbians have boys' names? She'd asked Jerri, one evening in her new apartment in Brooklyn, shortly after she'd left her husband, Phillip.

Do many lesbians have boys' names? Jerri asked. She was on the floor beside the stereo, picking out yet another Phoebe Snow album.

Yes, said Anne, then stopped short, and laughed. I suddenly wonder if Anne might not be short for Andrew.

Could be, said Jerri. Every man plans first for a son.

Jerri was the most beautiful woman Anne had seen, since it had dawned on her that a woman might also be made love to, deeply kissed. Large, soft dark eyes that missed nothing, perfect skin (not perfect, Jerri would protest, I got my share of pimples like everyone else); a lovely mouth, both vulnerable and strong. She was utterly 'butch.' Never wore skirts (Anne agreed she would look odd in them), short hair, the works. She fixed cars for a living. They had met because one morning Anne's car wouldn't start, and she'd called 'Mechanical Women, Car Specialists.' Jerri and her lover/partner Maude, had arrived, as Phillip stood on the stoop, briefcase in hand, on his way to the office.

I hope you know what you're doing, he'd said. Not judgmental. He really hoped it.

Men make me feel so dumb, she'd groaned, standing there with the women. I go in with the car and they ignore me for as long as there are other men bringing in their cars; then when they finally get to me you'd think nobody else's car ever broke down. And they call me honey. Which is worse than being ignored.

Well you did have the car towed in for service when it was only out of gas, said Phillip.

And you and those male mechanics will never forget it! she said.

The two women mechanics, after checking under the hood and muttering to each other, had placed themselves on large wood trays with wheels and swooshed themselves under her car. In a matter of minutes they had it going.

Phillip smiled down at the three of them and the three of them smiled up (the mechanics bored, businesslike; she archly, tickled) and she felt herself across a line from him.

We can do it! she thought.

Later Jerri told her that she and her lover, Maude, had thought she was a nerd.

I was so *proud* of you all, she said, walking over to the stereo, putting on the record Jerri handed up. And you were so *beautiful*, I couldn't believe it. I was brought up to think all beautiful women have long hair, you know. She laughed. And that you have to wear clingy dresses and delicate little shoes. And you never, never know anything about cars beyond how to drive them.

You fell in love with competence, said Jerri, with a shrug. That's why women like you fall in love with men. If women were as competent as men you wouldn't give men a second look. Not even a first.

No kidding, said Anne.

No kidding, Jerri had said, giving her a kiss. Competent as anything.

Conscious Birth

Black women are being murdered in Boston, Massachussetts.

White women are being murdered in California.

Native American women are being murdered in New Mexico.

Hispanic women are being murdered in New York.

Chicana women are being murdered in Texas.

All of us are being attacked because we are women, and no one really cares about us but us.

Let us understand this, and stop expecting the same Patriarchy that is killing us, to help save our lives. Refuse the role of victim! Create a new role and identity as fighters for Our Life!

*I send you my love, and my support, and my strong
clenched fist.*

In Sisterhood,

Anne Gray

She sent off this letter to a women's group in
Kentucky. A woman, met at one of her lectures, had
written asking for a statement of support. Saying 'Bucolic
Lexington' was now experiencing attacks on women
'epidemically.'

She wrote the letter of support: questioning, however,
the love, if not 'the strong clenched fist.' It was the word
'now.' Because her mind was always preoccupied to
some degree with the lives of Native American and
African women in the Americas during earlier centuries,
she found herself musing on the daily attacks on these
women, *then.* Was being sold to someone who raped and
beat you seen as an attack? Was having your village
torched and your children murdered seen as an attack, or
what? This was the part of Anne Gray's mind that could
become so strident and bitter that it could easily capsize
her. She'd given it a name: Grandma. So now she said,
sternly, Cut the shit, Grandma. This shit's not helpful, to
me personally, just at the moment. Thank you. Hearing a
door fly open with a bang, somewhere behind her in the
house, she spoke again. You know I don't mean any

disrespect, but, Life being what it is, I've got to just limp along here as best I can in the present, pretty much making it up as I go along. She sat still a moment, waiting. The house remained quiet. The banging door closed itself.

Thank you, she said again.

Still, all day long the letter nagged her. Who was this woman writing to her? Someone she'd met but did not remember. Was she white or black? White, most likely. And why had she wanted her support, her statement? Because she was a feminist. More than likely because she was black. And if that was the reason, then undoubtedly these white women against violence against women were seeking not to be seen as only white women. And she wondered if there were not black men somewhere in the murkiness of all this—and the white women not wanting to appear racist, but intent, nonetheless, on asserting their right to exist, unmolested. She cheered them. And yet, she thought: how easy it will be for all the attention to focus on black males, their violence, their general unruliness, because that is simply how America responds to its white damsels in distress; even though the majority of rapists, killers and whatnot are white men. And have been, in this country, on this continent, for the last 500 years. White men, of course, control the media. They are notoriously kind to themselves.

She worried the woman's letter, and her response to it,

for hours, for days: working, reading, walking, with it always at the back of her mind. So that when she heard that the Klan had opened fire on anti-Klan demonstrators in Greensboro, North Carolina, she felt guilt that she had perhaps, by writing her letter, made black men's lives—and women's: ironic how this still came as an afterthought; more ironic when she learned no black men were killed, only white men and one black woman—that much more vulnerable to attack. And yet, she must support women. She must support herself: the black and female self. And also The People, of which she was part, was, as woman, half.

More than half. Grandma chimed in.

Anne Gray had a wonderful sense of Grandma, and whenever she spoke, she saw her with perfect clarity. She was very dark brown, her face creased, her mouth 'chuned' up, a word Grandma herself used to describe the way an old person held her mouth after she'd lost all her teeth. Her head rag was worn low over her brow, nearly covering her wise, fed-up, take no prisoners and no bullshit neither eyes. She was slender, and walked slowly with a cane, with which she would hit you, likely as not, if you tried to act dirty. She even had a smell, like earth and greens and roses. And maybe a bit of liniment that she used for her arthritis. Anne loved her, and would sometimes laugh at how lucky she was to have her, and the fact that she and Grandma 'went everywhere together!'

So with Grandma along, though sulky from having been asked to lie low, Anne Gray continued her day, thoughts of complicity, assertiveness, guilt, crowding her: to speak out provoked violence; to remain silent encouraged death. It was a dilemma not at all new to people of color, or women.

Or even to good white men, too, said Grandma, grudgingly, but determined to be fair.

When her daughter arrived home with new roller skates and offered a demonstration, Anne Gray was relieved.

Half an hour later, having watched her daughter skate down the hall, leaving tracks in the carpet, and having, wobbly, tried the skates herself, it was time to cook dinner.

The cracked crab had been waiting on a shelf in the refrigerator all afternoon. She took it out and placed it in the crab pot to steam. Next she began to parboil a bowl of green beans and to wash lettuce for a salad. She located the local jazz station on the radio in the kitchen and listened to music. While the beans boiled, she made a quick study of the covers of *Freedomways* and *Callaloo*, magazines that lay unopened on the coffee table. All the time her mind was busy: The *Abalone Alliance* newsletter lay on the counter near the small pile of stems from the stringbeans. It proclaimed against the new Trident submarine (they named it after chewing gum, the bastards, she thought; to make it appear harmless, familiar: she had forgotten the God of the Deep, Poseidon), against the continued escalation of the arms race, between the Soviet Union and the United States. She read:

In August, 1945, the nuclear age began in pain and horror with the destruction of two Japanese cities. In the thirty-four years since, we have come to tolerate a vast military-industrial machine in our midst—a machine that siphons off our resources and produces only the devices of mass death.

The United States now has 30,000 nuclear weapons—equivalent to eight billion tons of T.N.T. These figures numb the mind and stagger the imagination. But the momentum of the military machine keeps building. It builds Missile-X and Trident in the name of security, and we grow ever less secure in an increasingly deadly world.

Individually we can do little but despair. Collectively, we have the power to act. Stopping the arms race is undeniably difficult, and may require transforming the political and social structures that support it. But we cannot build a free society on nuclear ruins.

Every time they raped me, said Grandma, muttering over Anne Gray's shoulder, I said that if they had the power they would blow up the earth. Hate rules them. And they know that they are the only ones down here on earth, to fear.

We can't build anything on nuclear ruins, Anne Gray thought. And yet, as yet, she was paralyzed, inactive, against the huge nuclear military machine. Had not marched against nuclear anything since the early Sixties. Then she had marched, had gone to Russia itself to express horror at the nuclear future that by now had caught up with them. Her daughter's primary fear was that the world would blow up. Her greatest fear, as a child her daughter's age, had been of being lynched, burned out, by mobs of white men, their women and children crowding around eager and curious during and after the act. At least she could conceive of a place—up North, she had thought—where these mobs of her nightmares could not reach; but not so, her child, who had never known the earth as stable, timeless—her child was unable to make any assumptions whatsoever about the planet. It seemed to shift under her feet.

Anne and Grandma peeked into the crab pot. Anne poked at the beans.

She felt her head inclining toward the comfort of Grandma's shoulder; she wished she had time to sit herself in Grandma's receptive lap. Surely there was simply too much to think about. The world was ending, possibly. Probably. And all the people who had no power individually, and who could not get together collectively, were prisoners of those who had power and the unity of their money; and we would all be destroyed together. She resented this most of all.

She began to set the table in this mood. So that when she heard her lover's key in the lock, she made a conscious effort to shake off an incipient depression. She remembered Toni Cade Bambara's statement that Depression Is Collaboration with the Enemy.

Her lover was brown and jovial, seeming to bounce— when he was happy, as he was tonight—when he walked. Having liberated himself from a marriage that no longer fit, he had the polished, just born look of the recently freed. Middle age looked good on him. He drew political cartoons for a living, and could always be counted on to recognize the humorous. Hugging her, he grabbed her butt, and lifted her tight against him. 'Is that crab I smell steaming, baby,' he asked, 'or is that you?'

This was the side of him that Grandma especially liked. She was sensual and very earthy, herself. Going, as she liked to say, way back.

'Did you know,' he said, over dinner, 'that there's a place in North Dakota, or is it South? Anyway, a place where they are mining uranium. (Usual suspects, said

Grandma.) The Indians, whose land it is of course, say that this spot they're digging in is the most sacred of all. And the most taboo. Because they consider it their mother's heart. According to legend, when a certain depth is reached, it means the death of the world.'

'And they're right,' she said. Though she thought this place was in Arizona.

Jason was angry that more black people did not join the anti-nuke movement. He did quite a number of cartoons admonishing them. Angry too that more feminists did not see it as a women's issue.

'Give us a break,' said Anne. 'Of course it's a black and women's issue, but black folks anyway are preoccupied with day-to-day survival. Our neighborhoods are being destroyed, for instance, so that affluent whites can move back into the city—which they left twenty years ago because *we* were coming.'

Sometimes these people tickle me, said Grandma. Always trying to keep us out of their neighborhoods. I bet it was a big surprise to them that they can't keep out cancer.

'But all neighborhoods are in danger,' said Jason.

Anne wondered if this meant white people now understood about precariousness. She doubted it.

She marveled at the mundane fact that she and her lover now sat like Mom and Pop at opposite ends of a familiar table, and were lovers and *compañeros* publicly.

Their old lives had eventually—with their acquiesence and even help—expelled them, like a mother giving birth. Being children of the Sixties, they had opted for conscious delivery.

They had rented a cabin near the coast, down the road a bit from Big Sur. She, her lover, her lover's wife, Suni, and their small child. She had written Suni a letter saying yes, perhaps they could be sisters, which was a reply to Suni's opinion that perhaps sisterhood was possible between them, and might even involve sitting outdoors on the steps in the evening braiding each other's hair. This was a romantic notion, but a gallant one; besides, as children of the Sixties, the unromantic didn't appeal to them, or even seem to apply. However, once actually at the site of the experiment: Can a lover and a wife explore being sisters if the man they both love is seriously freaking out?, the reality of simple co-existence sobered them all, considerably.

'I often wondered what you saw in him,' said Suni, speaking of Anne's husband. She was still married to Phillip, though separated, and beginning to see, like Suni herself, other women. To hear this from Suni startled her. No one had ever questioned her marriage to Phillip in just this way. They questioned why she married a white man—to which her reply was sometimes, Is he white?—but never what she'd seen in Phillip himself.

What she'd seen in Phillip was only too apparent, she had thought: he was good looking, warm, intelligent, and committed to the struggle for justice for black people—the last a major requirement for all her men, lovers as well as friends.

Suni, a small white woman with red hair and green eyes, pale freckled skin and frequently chapped lips, walked with her head down, surveying the pebbles in the logging trail they were on. She seemed to be always stooping to pick up something.

Though Jason and Anne spent nearly every night together across the hall from where Suni slept with the baby, she had demanded certain times in which to be alone with each of them; her own lover, a woman, was back in the city. (How Sixties it all was! They would laughingly say to each other, twenty years later.) The night before, she had slept with Jason. Anne was trying desperately to keep from thinking about it, but found it impossible.

'What did you do together?' she asked, flushing. Because each night she and Jason had made passionate love on the floor (the bed squeaked) beside the bed.

'I held him,' said Suni. 'Then he held me.'

'What do you do on other nights?'

'I take care of myself,' said Suni, 'which I enjoy doing sometimes.' She did not say: 'I thought of the two of you together and it excited me fiercely,' which was true.

She was attracted to Anne. And had told her so. She knew Anne was attracted to her, though she knew the feeling made Anne uncomfortable. They seemed to be attracted to each other *through* Jason, somehow, and this disturbed and puzzled them.

Anne had never seen what Jason saw in Suni, either. Though what he saw in her was exactly what she had seen in Phillip. Suni was attractive, intelligent, passionate about what she cared about, committed to the struggle to change society. She was incredibly and admirably dedicated to eradicating any racism she found lurking within herself. A difficult and ongoing battle, because she'd been raised by rich, Republican parents to remain perfectly white until the day she died, and she would have been, were it not for a summer spent teaching black children in Mississippi, and the awareness, while there, that a black 'Grandma,' similar to the one that lived in Anne's consciousness, lived in hers also. She was so white a white woman, she sometimes said, that she even seemed like a white woman to herself. This discovery had shocked her profoundly.

She'd laughed, telling Anne about her Grandma. 'The first time she started speaking I was walking over to the local rib joint in Tupelo, Mississippi, hoping to buy a fish sandwich. They had fish on Fridays. And Grandma said, just as clear: "Are you sure white girls eat this kind of fish?"'

Anne laughed.

'I stopped right in the middle of the road. I looked around. I said "Huh?" And she kept on talking, really making fun of me, but in a kind of easygoing way. And I finally got it, that she was inside my mind.'

'Yes,' said Anne.

'Hallelujah!' said Suni, grinning. 'Girl, I hadn't looked back since.'

'Well, you see,' said Anne, sitting down on a convenient log alongside the trail. 'I fell in love with Phillip. Besides, black men like Jason, who were of interest to me, were busy sampling elsewhere.' She smiled, but it was surprisingly bitter, considering.

'But he loved you, black men loved black women, all the time!' said Suni. 'His loving me didn't mean he stopped loving you all.'

'I knew that by the way he was there beside me every day,' said Anne, sardonically.

'But your husband, Phillip, was beside you every day,' said Suni, exasperated. 'A white man, remember? What did you want, both of them?'

Anne laughed. 'Maybe,' she said. Because it seemed to her that that is what white women had. Their own men and hers if they wanted him. She said this aloud. To which Suni snorted. 'But that's what you had. Your own man—even though he was with me, you didn't just drop out of his universe—and (she could not say 'my man' since she hated to think of white men as connected to her) a white man.'

How humiliating that their lives were so affected by men in general and by Jason in particular. Simply to cease thinking about men and to run off with each other was a thought that delighted some part of both of them. It would serve men, Jason for instance, right. And yet, the freedom of that choice, at least to Anne, was largely illusory. It was only her femaleness that she felt she related to in Suni. Her whiteness (not the color itself but the attitudes developed because of it, no matter how assiduously Suni sought to tame herself) she could not abide.

Arrogance: 'I feel secure in my marriage,' she said. 'Jason always comes back to me.'

Which meant that, as a black woman, Anne had no chance at all of winning him away.

And of course she preferred to think 'winning him away' was the farthest thing from her mind.

'You not fooling no one but yourself,' said Grandma.

And so she had 'won' him away and they had spent a decade and a half deconstructing every impediment to their intimacy. Racism and colorism were scrutinized. Sexism confronted head-on. Classism studied as if in a class. At the end of this process, which taught them more than could be imagined prior to daring it, they realized they had other areas of study elsewhere, and with other mates. Twenty years later Jason was happily married to someone else, not either of them!

Suni was deep into spirituality and followed a guru, and Anne was having a passionate though platonic affair with a very young boy. A man, but young, boyish.

The minute he walked into my house I knew something was up, said Anne.

She was driving them to the local ashram and was looking forward to meeting, or at least hearing, Suni's guru.

Suni turned to her expectantly.

He was sooo *cute*! said Anne. He'd come to see someone who used to live in our house, a former classmate. That person was long since gone; I'd lived in the house nine years. Still, we seemed to be who we were both really expecting to see. He sort of rocked back on his heels. I stood in the doorway staring at him as if I'd seen a ghost. I couldn't have explained it then. I thought it was just how dear he looked. A smallish young man. Big dark eyes, a guileless grin. Nice teeth. Curly, curly hair. Less than half my age.

I think you turn here, said Suni, as they approached a light.

Right, said Anne.

All my cells sort of woke up.

Wow, said Suni, that's how I felt the first time I heard

Gurumayi. I didn't even see her. A friend gave me a tape of a talk she gave at the ashram last year. It felt like water to my desert. I hadn't realized how arid I was. How stuck and sort of floundering.

I know, said Anne. Isn't it the pits? How we go along feeling half alive sometimes; not even half.

We're asleep, said Suni. Just walking and talking, eating and shitting. Sound asleep.

And we have to be that way, of course, said Anne. It's the human equivalent of fallowness.

Spiritual hibernation, said Suni.

But I hated it, said Anne. I used to hate it so much; it was such a state of numbness, interspersed of course with cliff-hanging depressions; I was tempted to try to reconnect with Jason. But every time we talked about maybe getting back together, I burst into tears. We'd burned all our material. Every scrap of the stuff we needed to do together.

That's the great thing about Jason, said Suni, remembering her marriage. You could finish your stuff with him.

It is a good thing, isn't it? I have had lovers and friends you couldn't finish anything with. Old shit just kept hanging and hanging. She made a wry face at this repugnant description.

Suni made a disgusted sound.

*

The first time I saw Gurumayi I fell in love with her, she said. She was so beautiful, and so young! She looked like a girl.

I never knew there were women gurus, said Anne.

Neither did I, said Suni. But when I saw her, I thought: Of course. How natural. For sure I wouldn't have been as interested in listening to a man. And she's teaching me so much about what's important. Happiness. Compassion. Ecology of the soul. How meditation is as necessary as changing your bed linen and flossing.

I can't believe how life keeps pulling back the veil! said Anne.

What's his name? asked Suni.

Adam, of course, said Anne, laughing.

What's so funny? asked Suni.

It's just perfect, that after all these years Life sends me a man to love who doesn't seem to have any kind of baggage. It isn't sexual between us, it isn't romantic, he doesn't need me to provide housing. He rides a bicycle everywhere. In a way, he feels like my first man.

Is he gay? asked Suni.

I've no idea, said Anne. He's certainly *fun*. I've danced more with Adam than I've danced with anyone in my whole life. Listened to more music. Gone on more bike rides. Sometimes I feel so happy with him I have to ask myself: How did this happen? What does it mean?

You should see a psychic, said Suni.

There was a long pause while both women concentrated on the traffic that swirled around them and the cozily lit shops lining San Pablo Avenue.

It wasn't as mysterious as I'd thought, said Anne, almost under her breath. She wasn't sure she should say this to Suni who, in the old days, according anyway to Jason, had taken a dim view of things supernatural. No. I believe Adam and I have known each other a long time. Maybe always. That he is my soul's recognition of a child I aborted twenty-five years ago.

Really, said Suni, interested.

Yes, said Anne. I had the longest talk with the spirit of that child, after I let it go. I didn't know enough and was too scared and desperate anyway to talk to it *before* I let it go. I was barely out of my teens. Quite ignorant. But over the years, as I've understood more, I've wanted to connect with it. Not so much to apologize, but to explain my terrified and impoverished circumstances, the fact that I was abandoned by his father, who was also young and scared, and to express my grief and love. He had a beautiful little spirit. I have imagined him in every stage as he was growing, or would have been growing, up. He would have been named Adam, too.

Something serious is going on in the Universe, said Suni, thoughtfully.

Yes, said Anne. And one of the most serious things for me has been the understanding that the Universe is not that interested in punishing us. Every move we make is simply part of its reflection.

I'd always heard 'You must be careful what you ask for,' said Suni. But I didn't understand it, except, maybe, negatively. But really, Life is definitely open to giving you whatever you sincerely ask for. Though maybe not in a form you can immediately recognize it in.

You know, she said, how I am always collecting things that I find on the ground.

Yes, said Anne. That's an image of you that stays with anyone who's known you for long.

Ah, yes, said Suni. Jason used to make me put shells back in the ocean, after I'd collected so many you could barely find a spot to put your coffee cup in our house. He said it was very white. Collecting. Grabbing. Hoarding. Leaving the earth bare. She shuddered. It was a hard thing to have a black man say to me, even if he was my husband.

Anne was quiet. It had started to rain. The swish of the wipers seemed sudden and loud. She was glad she'd gotten up the nerve to call Suni, after all these years, and pleased that Suni had agreed to see her. She thought of how precious it was to be able to know another person over many years. There was an incomparable richness in it.

So I started to think about it, and to limit my grabbing. I learned to find things, beautiful things, and not need to take them home. And then, recently, I've wanted to find a shark's tooth. And every day on my walk along the beach I've looked for one. Now mind you, the shark's tooth I had in mind was perfect: big, yellow, sharp. A majestic shark's tooth.

And what did you find? asked Anne, laughing.

The most gnarly, rat's ass of a shark's tooth one could imagine. She laughed. But it was a shark's tooth.

And what did you do with it? asked Anne. Fling it back?

Not on your life, said Suni, bringing the blunted, dark old thing from under her jacket, where it hung around her neck from a golden chain. If this is the shark's tooth Life wants me to have, then by golly, this is the shark's tooth I bloody well want!

Anne felt very close to Suni in this moment. She reached over and clasped her hand. Suni squeezed her fingers absentmindedly, but warmly, still laughing.

Some people nowadays try to make women feel guilty for having had abortions, Anne said finally. They claim the aborted fetuses are wrathful and want to harm the women who aborted them. The spirit of my child has felt just the opposite. I've felt his yearning to comfort me, to love and cherish me. To make me smile.

You think Adam sent Adam! said Suni.

I do, said Anne. Or rather, I think Life sent Adam. And why would Life do that? Send me a delightful young male spirit that I instantly recognized? Because Life was out there preparing such a Being for Its own purpose. But because I can appreciate what Life created, and sincerely grieved its absence in my life, I get to enjoy it when Life, *drylongso*, just doing Its Thang, shoots it my way.

What has Grandma had to say about it? asked Suni.

Grandma is thrilled, she said, as they parked in the ashram parking lot, Grandma and I both love to dance.

This Is How It Happened

This Is How It Happened

This is how it happened. After many years of being happier than anyone we knew, which worried me, my partner of a dozen years and I broke up. I still loved him, in a deeply familial way, but the moments of palpable deadness occurring with ever greater frequency in our relationship warned me we'd reached the end of our mutual growth. How to end it? How to get away?

My old friend Marissa, with whom I'd been infatuated years ago in Brooklyn, came to San Francisco for a visit. She was a dyke, pure and strange, and I could never see her without a certain amount of awe. She was the most beautiful of women, shapely and brown, but she could also wire houses and fix cars. All the while speaking in the softest of voices and never showing any of her innate wildness until left alone on the dance floor. She immediately caused the other dancers to disappear and the dance floor itself to retreat until it seemed to be in a forest somewhere and the 5000 or so years of a lackluster patriarchy fairly forgotten.

We had met while I was in a marriage with a decent, honorable man who had not danced in six or seven years, and she was living with a woman who told her what to eat, think and wear. I didn't know this when we met, of course. Because she was an electrician and earned her own living I found her strong, independent, free. In retrospect we decided, once we'd been separated for some years from our earlier partners, we'd been infatuated with the image of each other that we needed to help us flee.

'I thought you always knew exactly what you were doing,' she said. 'To have married someone nice to support you while you perfected your craft as an artist. To have had children with someone who supported you and them. Oh,' she continued, 'the list was long.'

I was amazed. 'It was all instinct,' I said. 'I had seen so many women married to men who squashed their development. Any hint of such a personality turned me off. And of course,' I said, 'I never seriously considered women.' Nor had I understood I could.

'Well,' she said, 'you wouldn't have done any better with the one I found. Libby is just the man her father was. Domineering, bossy, a real pain in the neck.' She sighed. 'And after the first couple of years, no sex.'

'No sex?' How could sexy Marissa not be having sex?

Marissa shrugged. 'It's a curious thing to encounter the father of your woman leering out at you. Which is what happened when Libby drank. She'd forget we'd argued and that I'd been humiliated over some outrageous behavior of hers. She'd get sentimental in her drunkenness and want to make love. By force if necessary. I was repelled.'

I too had enjoyed making love with Tripper for many years. Then it seemed to me my sexual rhythm was broken. I no longer experienced any periods of horniness, as I had earlier in my life. Eventually I realized it was because over time Tripper's sexual needs set the times of love's occasions. I was never able to say no, but my body did. It withheld its pleasure, since its own desire was not permitted to set the pattern of celebration and release.

Why didn't either of us speak up? Marissa and I often asked each other. We agreed that we'd tried, but habits, once formed, had proved hard to break, and retreat and silence had offered a spuriously virtuous comfort. Our mothers' behavior, probably, copied while we were very young, too early to recognize it for the depression it was.

The week I left Tripper he was still interested in making love to me, and suggested a goodbye 'fuck' even though my body had not for many months expressed the slightest desire. In fact, it had expressed just the opposite, with its pancake flat nipples, and a vulva so dry I'd thought I'd prematurely entered 'the change.'

When Marissa came to pick me up Chung was in the kitchen attempting to repair the toaster. His straight black hair, with the dapper streak of gray on the left side, hung in his eyes, and his somewhat paunchy torso, sans shirt, glistened with sweat. When we'd met I'd practically drooled over his body. I still admired it, but in a more critical way. I loved the fact that he was short, and that when we kissed, we could look squarely into each other's eyes. Also that my arms reached easily around him—Tripper had been both large and tall—and I could grab a nice handful of his butt. Marissa took beer from the fridge and sat gap-legged at the table sipping it and watching him struggle with the toaster as long as she could stand it. By the time I was ready to go she'd ripped it from his fingers and declared it dead and therefore inefficient. Chung, who has a sense of humor if not much vitality at this stage in his life, grabbed a beer for himself and was still laughing as we went out of the house.

I backed my battered pea green Karman Ghia out of the driveway and then stopped to put down the top. Marissa and I flew down the streets giddy as teenagers, serene as the old friends we were.

At the dance, as I suspected, Marissa was queen. The

best dancers sought her out and she outdanced all of them. It was the kind of dyky joint that still intimidated me. The kind with lots of women in all manner of dress and an obligatory three or four men. I was always wondering about the men. Who were they? Why were they there? Were they bouncers? Were they brothers of some of the women? Lovers of some of the women? Straight? Bisexual? Gay?

What men? was always Marissa's response when I asked her about them.

Tonight as always I sat quietly in a corner hoping not to be approached. Unless it was by a particular woman across the room who attracted me by the sexiness of her dress—I liked femme-looking women I'd discovered, with their low-cut dresses and light, pinky-plum colors. But butches too—like Marissa, who wore tight jeans, a leather jacket and a scarf around her neck—could be almost unbelievably alluring. Marissa would dance with me until my lack of wildness bored her. Then she'd whirl out on the dance floor dancing only with women who, in their abandon, reminded her of herself. Or, she'd dance alone, a voluptuous brown-skinned woman with dread-locks to her ass, and everyone watching her imagined her dancing just for them, in silvery moonlight beneath a canopy of ancient trees, naked.

After sleeping together once or twice why hadn't we become lovers? I often asked myself. Perhaps because you can't recall whether it was once or twice, said Marissa, when I queried her. I certainly loved and admired her. Yet she seemed somehow beyond me, freer. I felt I'd never catch up. Her way seemed natural to her. I would have to learn it. This frightened, irritated and depressed me. I tried to imagine Marissa in a hetero-sexual relationship and it made me laugh. I tried to imagine the two of us as a couple and it made me uneasy.

Sitting in my corner drinking a margarita I was for a moment unaware I'd been watching a woman standing by the door holding a baby in her arms. This was so incongruous: the loud music, the energetic dancing, the drinking and smoking, that I immediately rose and walked over to her, offering her the seat next to mine. She could not come over just yet, she explained, because she was selling some articles of apparel from Guatemala which I now noticed she carried in a large denim bag at her feet. I was shocked by this, I don't know why. But within minutes I was holding the baby, a fitfully dozing black-eyed boy, who was not an infant but a two-year-old, and she was squatting beside her merchandise where much to my surprise she seemed to make sales by simply rummaging for a particular item in her bag and then briefly flinging it over a cleared spot on the floor. Money changed hands rapidly and soon she'd sold enough colorfully striped cotton trousers, headbands and vests to satisfy her for the evening. Dragging what was left in her bag she hurried over to us. The baby strained against my arms as she approached, and resolutely wriggled off my lap and toddled up to her. When they met, on the fringe of the whirling dancers, who any minute I expected to stomp on him, she smiled down at him and stopped to swing him up in her arms. At that moment the Drifters or some other old group was singing the golden oldie 'With Every Beat of My Heart,' and the two of them danced a moment cheek to cheek. Her hair was in short, thick, warrior erect dreadlocks. She was wearing pants that looked like a skirt, and a light blue denim shirt with an open collar. Beneath the shirt was a peach-colored tank. She wore earrings. Bracelets. And on her feet, sturdy brown boots.

It happened in the moment they were dancing, the child closing his eyes in a swoon of delight. The woman a being I'd never seen before.

The Brotherhood of the Saved

I did not know what the Brotherhood of the Saved had told her, but I knew they had told her something. She was sitting very straight in the green porch swing, as if prepared to do battle. I suddenly noticed that her eyes, which looked at me shrewdly, were old, and that the light in them was half of what it used to be. She was, otherwise, her usual stout and jaunty self, wearing a neatly ironed housedress and a pair of faded green flip-flops.

Hello Mama, I said.

Is that my daughter? she replied, her usual response. Except that now it seemed more of a legitimate question. As if she really wondered.

It's me, I said, moving toward her and leaning down to kiss her forehead.

There were deep wrinkles across her brow. In a moment of vanity I wondered if I would have them when I reached her age. If I ever, in fact, did so.

We have great genes, she used to say, before mine began to be expressed in a problematic way. We don't show our age until we die.

This always made me laugh, though she swore it was true.

That was before the ozone layer began to disappear, of course. Now we seemed to wrinkle at the same rate as everyone else.

Pretty hot, isn't it, I said, taking a seat in the swing beside her.

It sure is, she said, in the way that Southerners comment on hot weather as if its hotness is a daily surprise.

How's the patient? I asked, taking her left arm and beginning to gently manipulate it at the elbow.

You know, she said, I never would have believed it possible, but every bit of the pain and swelling was gone by the time you left the driveway yesterday.

I smiled, and asked her to make a fist.

Around here people think a chiropractor is just some kind of quack, she said. Out to get people's money without doing them any good.

It works, I said.

How did you say you found out about it? she asked.

She always forgot this, no matter how many times I told her.

I learned the hard way, I said. I was always getting sports injuries.

Oh, that's right, she said. Even as a little child you were the one to be falling out of trees.

That's how I broke my arm, remember?

Oh, I remember, alright. She thought about it for a minute. That didn't stop you from climbing trees though. It sure didn't.

Sitting there beside her, forty-five years old and ready to begin the second half of my life, I wondered why it hadn't.

You were willful and stubborn, my mother said, reading my mind.

I shrugged. I loved trees and I loved a good high view, I said. Still do.

Um-hum, she said.

In high school I got banged up a lot, but in college is where I really got creamed.

They didn't want girls playing; and especially not playing like a boy.

I wasn't playing like a boy. I was playing like myself.

Too good, she said, grunting.

So what is the Brotherhood of the Saved saying about me now? I asked.

She paused. The foot that kept the swing moving was still.

You really want to know? she asked.

Yep, I said.

That you're a sinner and bound for hell, she said, with a sigh.

They've been saying that for a while, I said. Nothing new they got? I asked.

They also say that what you do with women is a crime.

You mean sleep with them?

Yes.

Well, I said, pushing the swing so that it rocked a bit to the left, If sleeping with women is a crime it's one for which the whole world is guilty.

What you mean? she asked, startled.

I mean everybody on earth has slept with a woman, even the two or three who started life in a petri dish.

She still looked puzzled.

You came here sleeping not only with a woman but inside one, I said.

Oh, she said.

It's stupid to think sleeping with women is wrong, I said. What kind of jackass would have that opinion?

Yes, but you know what they mean, she said.

Oh yes, I said, SEX, the four-letter word. They can't believe it can be enjoyed without a penis.

Trane, she said, using the nickname she herself gave me because I loved John Coltrane's music so much when I was growing up.

I wish these hypocrites would get a life! I said. They're dying to see women sleep with each other. It accounts for half of the pornography they buy.

Oh, she said, the Brothers don't watch that stuff!

How do you know? I asked. It's available in every hotel they're likely to spend any time in. It's all over the newsstands and on the street. How do you think they keep up the passion to rail against it? If they weren't watching it and getting turned on by it, they wouldn't just automatically think of women doin' each other first thing in the morning. They might instead be thinking of cirrhosis of the liver or heart disease. Crime in the streets. Poverty in the hinterland. The way the weather is all screwed up. What's really going on.

I've never watched it, she said. Smug.

No, I said, you're afraid.

Why am I afraid, she asked, after a long moment during which the swing's creaking was the only sound.

Oh, I said, so you admit it. I put my arm around her.

With you I seem to be able to admit anything, she said, with surprise. The more they try to make me not like you, the more lonely I feel.

That's good, I said.

You're a strange creature, though, she said.

Must be because of genes, I said.

*

Miss Mary was wearing a hat that appeared to support a complete crop of cherries. On top of her jet black wig. An ancient boater, the rest of it was made of straw and looked like something you'd only see in movies. Movies in which frivolous people flopped about on the dance floor. Or threw picnics in artificial wildernesses. A few local indigenous in the background looking impressed and eager to offer service. Beneath it, however, she wore a black Gap T-shirt, black pedal pushers and a pair of chartreuse espadrilles. Miss Mary had always had a sense of style and I commented on it now.

Wow, I said. If seventy looks like this, eighty must look fabulous.

Who said I'm seventy? she asked, looking at me over her aerospace-style glasses.

Now, Girl, said my mother, who was also wearing a hat I wouldn't have believed she owned. A huge white thing made of something very deceased, with a big pink bow on the side. It reeked of mothballs.

Auntie Fanny's hat outdid both my mother's and Miss Mary's. It was black and intensely dramatic, larger than theirs by inches, and with a leopard's tail somehow coiling down the side.

I was wearing a baseball cap turned backward. Miss Mary tugged on one of my doo-doo braids.

Girl, when you going to do something about your hair. It looks like you platted it yourself.

I did, I said. Thinking how, until I went to school, I thought platted was a real word.

You'd better turn that thing around, said my mother.

Why? I asked, as we drove into the parking lot of the newest of Atlanta's sleaze malls.

Someone might recognize you!

Yeah, I said, but probably not before I recognized them.

I noticed all three women had slid down in their seats. From outside the car it would seem I was chauffeuring three immense hats around the mall.

Okay, I said, turning off the motor after parking in front of the theater, we're here.

Oh, God, said my mother.

Oh, stop it, said Miss Mary.

It's probably not that bad, said Auntie Fanny.

Yeah, said my mother. How bad can it be? I've seen childbirth. She let out a sigh of relief.

What's the name of this film? asked Miss Mary.

Deep Throat, I said.

Oh, said my mother, brightening. It's not even about down there. She sat up straighter in her seat and undid her seat belt.

Though it was three in the afternoon there was a long line. All men. I wondered how long it would take them to notice.

Gawd, said my mother, immediately, we're the only women here. She turned as if to get back into the car.

Miss Mary prodded her in the back with her purse. Keep stepping, she said.

Looking back at her I had to laugh. She was moving along like a very little girl, her eyes firmly closed. Led by my mother, whose back she was right up against.

Auntie Fanny had turned pale.

All these white men, she said. Makes it hard to breathe.

Yeah, said Miss Mary, get them suckers stirred up no telling what they might do.

I'm glad I let my hair go gray, said my mother, momentarily doffing her hat and using it as a fan.

That wouldn't stop 'em, muttered Auntie Fanny.

Never stopped 'em before, said Miss Mary.

Women, please, I said, turning around and passing them their tickets. Slavery is over, segregation too, and besides, I said, noting the sagging bellies of the men and their wimpy pecs, you could probably outrun all of them.

What are those young black men doing here? asked my mother, pointing.

Three black teenagers had pulled up and now dipped and bobbed to the back of the line.

I grabbed her finger. Didn't anybody ever teach you not to point, I said. It's not polite.

They have popcorn! she said in amazement as we entered the theater, ignoring me and wandering toward the bar.

*

I don't want to sit where anybody can see me, said Miss Mary. She had a gold tooth set in the side of her mouth. In the dimly lit theater it sparkled every time she spoke.

I want to sit near the door, said my mother. If it's too rough I can just slip out. Did you leave the car door unlocked? I could just wait for you all.

Mother, please, I said.

Okay, okay, she said. I still don't quite understand why the Good Lord sent me you, she grumbled.

To be sure you have a good seat, I said, steering them to seats near the back, by the exit.

Why way back here, complained Auntie Fanny, I'm too old to see way down there.

It's a big screen, I said. You'll see okay. Besides, anybody sitting behind you wouldn't be able to see over all that hat.

Oh, she said, with petulance.

About halfway through the film I thought all three of my ladies had died. It was that quiet. Suddenly abashed at the thought of bringing them to see such a nightmarish film, I peered guiltily over at them.

Dropped jaws. Buckets of popcorn still untouched. Auntie Fanny's overbuttered popcorn littering the floor.

The silence continued even after the film ended and we were back in the car.

Half an hour later and halfway back to their little town

of 1800 citizens: 900 'colored' and most of the rest white, I started to sing softly to myself. 'Love and Happiness,' by Al Green.

Stop that, said my mother.

Why? I asked. Does it bother you?

How can you be singing?

Yeah, said Miss Mary. I feel like I been to a funeral.

This the kind of stuff people watch nowadays? asked Auntie Fanny, her hat in her lap.

More and worse, I said.

And that woman acting like it was so good, said Miss Mary.

Oh, I said, she says they beat her to make her act that way.

What? said my mother.

The people who made the film, I said; she says the man who made her star in it, beat her to make her grin and bear it the way she does.

And she's a white woman? she asked. Or she just look that way.

Italian, I said. White enough.

They all turn white once they get here, said Miss Mary.

What are those things called when you, you know what? asked my mother.

When you you know what? I repeated softly.

You know, said Auntie Fanny.

Oh, I said. When you come.

Girl, hush. Said my mother.

Orgasm, I said, ignoring her. They're called orgasms.

No colored person thought up that word, that's for sure, said Auntie Fanny. Got a wormy sound to it. Gets slimy and hung up in your back teeth.

I laughed.

It's a trip being trapped in somebody else's language, isn't it, I said.

It sure is, said Miss Mary. Like, white people talk about 'vocation' when they mean job. She thought for a moment. I wonder if colored people ever had their own language, she said.

Sure thing, I said. Still do.

You know how much colored like to talk, said my mother. They'd have to.

There's a language in West Africa called Wolof, I said. The word for yes is 'wow.'

Sure 'nough? asked Auntie Fanny.

Yes, I said. I have a friend who speaks this language. Whenever I go to visit him I ask him to talk to me in Wolof for hours on end, even though 'wow' is the only word I understand. Every time he says it I want to kiss him.

I thought you didn't like mens, said Miss Mary.

Think again, I said. I just don't go for the disrespect, I said.

You got that right, said my mom. Then looked out the window as if she'd said too much.

Come is better than orgasm, said Auntie Fanny, thought-fully, and with conviction. Pussy is hotter than vagina. Though I guess you wouldn't want to have your doctor talking about pussy while you up on the examining table.

Why Fanny Johnson, said my mother, shocked.

We was all young once, said Miss Mary, firmly.

And I did like myself a good time, said Auntie Fanny. But just straight fucking, thank you very much. I didn't want nobody doing me like they done that poor thing in the film. I never wanted nothing going down my throat but food.

It's weird, isn't it? I offered.

Big ole nasty thing, said Auntie Fanny. And that man look like a retard.

You can't come in your throat, said Miss Mary. I don't care how what you call it, liberated, you get. They'd have to beat you to make you think that.

Exactly, I said.

Some women have a hard time coming no matter what you do.

Men, too, from the way that man next to us was wheezing and grunting.

Oh, that was so embarrassing, said my mother. I was glad he was white.

I was mortified, said Miss Mary.

I wanted to reach over, grab his hand, and tell him to hush.

Not his hand. Said Auntie Fanny. The whole place start to have a funny smell.

Well they're saying in the news that menfolks ain't what they used to be, said my mother.

How's that? asked Auntie Fanny.

They can't what do you call it . . . she said, trailing off.

Get it up, I said.

Girl, hush, she said.

Naw, and they can't make babies that good anymore either, said Miss Mary.

Well if they can't what do you . . .

Get it up . . . I said.

How they going to make any babies?

It's the beef, said Mom.

Not that they need to make any more, Miss Mary said. When you think they gon' notice this? All the time running around acting like all the world needs is more of them. You can tell they crazy.

I love babies myself, said my mother.

Okay, Mom, I said. Don't start. I could have had babies if I wanted them. You don't have to have a man to have a baby. You just have to have some sperm.

Girl, hush, she said.

What you going to take us to see next? asked my mom.

Three Girls a Dog and a Horse, I said, or *Mary and Sue*

Discover Right Action. Maybe next Thursday evening and maybe on video.

Oh, a kiddie film with animals, said Miss Mary, optimistically.

My mother's silence was stern.

I parked the car in front of our house.

Knowing Sister, here, said Miss Fanny, grimly, and poking the back of my neck, I wouldn't count on it.

I don't even want to see that, said my mother, if it has anything that could be nasty to animals in it.

What time? asked the other two.

What is it that you'd say is the most important thing about me? I asked my father.

He didn't hesitate for a moment.

That you're smart, he said.

Since we'd gone to Negril, Jamaica, together when I was experiencing my first or maybe second change of life, at the age of thirty-two, we seemed able to talk about anything.

On an impulse, and in what seemed to be a diversion from suicide, I'd called him and asked him to go with me.

He'd never gone anywhere before. I was amazed when he said: Well, send me a ticket.

We'd met at the airport in Montego Bay. He looked only mildly startled to be away from his house, and hugged me casually, as Southern fathers do when they greet their long-lost daughters in public.

What's wrong? he'd asked, after we'd settled into our shack-like beach house.

I love this place already, I said. What an ocean, what a view.

I can't swim, you know, he said.

I know, I said. That's partly why we came here, you can walk out for over a mile and still be walking.

Feet on the bottom? he asked. You sure?

Yes, I said. That man I married and I used to come here all the time. He was shocked that I'd have a toke and drift out to sea.

It sure is a major blue, he said.

Major blues, I said. I've never seen more beautiful water.

My father excused himself to put on something more comfortable.

I rummaged in my beach bag for my skimpy bathing suit.

In minutes we stood ready to take the plunge.

Half an hour later, after swimming underwater and enjoying the colors of the fish, I surfaced near him and said:

I think I'm losing my mind.

Oh, he said, surprised to see me so near and jumping back in alarm.

Yes, I said. I don't see how people stand to stay married

to one person for the whole of their lives.

That's not what you said when your mama and I got divorced.

It's not, I said. But I didn't know any better then. You'd been together the entire time I'd known you. I couldn't imagine my own life without the assurance that the two of you were living in the same house.

Houses get small, he said.

I'm hip, I said.

After he returned from Negril, my father moved from the shed out back behind my mother's house in town, and started living in a trailer on a plot of land he owned near the river. It wasn't much of a river, but he dug out the section in front of his trailer each dry season so that he now had a large fishing hole just outside his door.

He'd let his hair grow long, rasta style, and it was silvery white, the color of moth wings. Around his dark brown face it looked stunning. He'd learned to enjoy the occasional toke, as well, and had acquired a Rishi-like look of serenity in his eyes.

It's such a relief not to see people every day, he said, inviting me to sit on the porch he'd attached to the trailer and partially hidden behind bamboo.

Way back here, I said, do you ever see them?

Not unless I invite them. Though one time some census takers woke me up to inquire whether I was counted.

I laughed. And you said?

I said I didn't give a shit whether I was counted or not. After all, he said, I don't go around counting myself.

He paused.

Imagine. Trying to count everybody on earth. Just so they can make stuff to sell to them.

Dad, I said, Do you think I should keep fighting to keep Mom?

Save her from the Brotherhood? he asked.

Yes, I said.

Let's go see your Uncle Brother, he said.

Uncle Brother was my father's brother, and my uncle. So to me, he was Uncle Brother. He lived in the projects with his aged and nervous wife, Aunt BabySis.

Ho, BabySis, said my father when we arrived. How's Brother?

Tolerable, said Aunt BabySis. He rested some last night. An hour, maybe.

We entered the tiny bedroom on tiptoe. Uncle Brother lay propped up in bed staring just above the huge color television screen on which Ann Margaret was spread out like a flesh mountain. Without his glasses I wondered if he could even tell she was a woman. She was trying to sing something and then a man came into the bar where she was and grabbed her by the arm. Her hair flopped into her eyes and the next minute somebody else was offering her a beer. Then a car driven by some black-haired people crashed through the window.

How you doin'? asked my father.

Uncle Brother looked at my father, squinted slowly, and seemed to fix him in his sights.

Ho, he said. Brother. Busy dyin'.

BabySis said you rested some last night, said my father.

The Brotherhood and them came by and prayed over me, he said.

Hum, huh. Said my dad.

They do that every evening, said Aunt BabySis. Sure as clockwork.

Seem to do you good? asked my dad.

There was no reply from Uncle.

I slip him some valerian, I do, from time to time, said Aunt BabySis, meekly, in a whisper.

Dad looked at me.

I wonder what they pray about? I said.

He chuckled and an amused look crossed his face. One I remembered occurring frequently during my years of growing up. You always ask just the right thing! he would say with delight. For a moment I felt an intense surge of pity for my father. No matter what I did, it seemed, he couldn't help but like me. It shocked me to think his separation from my mother might have had something to do with me.

Uncle's tired eyes swung slowly upward in alarm. I saw them widen with fear.

Now, now, said my father. You've known Hannah since she was a tot. She's the same person. Just like your son.

The fear seemed to grow.

You all hear much from Harry? asked my father, patting Uncle's shoulder and looking behind him to see Aunt BabySis.

Well, you know how he is, said Aunt BabySis. He always love his daddy. He used to come all the time when he found out his daddy was sick. That was in the beginning. But his daddy chased him away. Got out of his sick bed to run him out of the yard. Yes he did. All I could do was cry.

You could have tied his sick old ass to the bed, said my father, jovially, squeezing Uncle's wasted arm. That's what you could have done.

Brother, hush. Said Aunt BabySis.

It was a sight, I can say that for it, said my father, on the way home.

I was staring out the window of his truck thinking about life in general.

You know, when we was growing up, no white people would even speak to you in a decent tone of voice if they saw you on the street. It was either fake polite or down-right mean. So to drive up to Brother's door and see all white people trailing into his sickroom. Well, it was a sight, for sure.

And these were white folks you all knew from before? I asked.

Yes, said Dad. We knew 'em when they was Methodists and Baptists. Pentecostals and Faith Healers. But now they're the Brotherhood, and they claim now they believe every man is created equal. Course, they didn't seem to know they could believe this till the laws changed.

And women? I asked.

Still don't talk much about that subject, said Dad.

He turned into the wild, overgrown lane that led to his paradise. I reached out the window to touch the branches of trees that scraped against the truck.

But women do come to pray? I asked.

Yes, they do, said my father. Old and young.

I tried to imagine it. What would it feel like, for an old colored man like Uncle who had grown up desperately afraid of white people to find them grouped round his bed as he lay dying.

I laughed.

What's funny? asked my dad.

It could be something out of Faulkner, I said.

Yes, said my dad. You know, I like to listen to him on tape.

I knew you would, I said. He had flaws, like we all do. But he was so miserable a lot of the time he couldn't help but tell the truth. I thought, but didn't say:

Faulkner, an alcoholic, wrote like a man with PMS.

You bring me anything else to listen to? asked my father.

Yes, I said. I brought you a tape about African medicine.

I bet it's different from the medicine here, said my dad.

They use a lot of herbs, I said.

That's what BabySis wants to use with Brother, he said. You hear her mention giving him valerian? But the Brotherhood is against it. Called it acting like a witch.

Oh, God, I said.

I heard 'em pray one time, he said, as he got out of the truck.

And? I said.

He laughed.

Oh, he said, you can imagine what they would sound like when they pray. Like they visualizing a real big *mean* somebody they hope can't visualize them back.

I laughed.

Brother was scared out of his mind, but didn't want to let on. He didn't want them to know they scared him. They'd finally come to try to do some good, bringing those young white girls too, so near to his bed, and all he could do was tremble. The idea of these white folks doing a poor black man good! I bet he wet himself.

So what's the scoop on Harry?

He went up North, the way so many of our children do.

Then people say the children leave because of the white folks. But Harry never would have left home if his daddy hadn't throwed him out.

Because he's gay?

I don't understand that kind of thing myself, he said, after a silence.

You want me to try to explain it? I asked.

Naw, he said. I don't feel like I'm quite old enough.

You're old enough, I said.

Not ready, then, he said.

There was a pause.

Life is funny though, he said. Got a sense of humor, sure as you please.

How's that?

Soon as segregation was finished, and the white folks was worried about the safety of their girls, Harry started being seen all over the place with one of the Brotherhood of the Saved's people's sons.

No. I said.

Yes, he said.

So how'd that play with the Brotherhood?

Oh, said Dad, the white boy eventually sickened and died, so his daddy felt some relief. But Harry didn't die, and for a long time didn't even leave town. You remember Harry. The children used to tease him and say he looked like a girl, but he was stubborn and as often as not could beat the shit out of them. I always liked him myself. But my brother said God wanted him to stay away from his own son, 'cause what he was doing with men was evil in His sight.

He paused, thoughtfully.

Well, he said, everybody always said I was a sinner, anyhow. Rather fish than do anything else on a Sunday, the only day the colored used to have off. I told Brother, Something must be wrong with God's eyes, if seeing Harry offended his sight. That boy was loyal as the day was long. Loved his folks.

So the two daddies have something in common to pray over, I said.

Shameful children, he grunted.

I don't wonder that Brother can't sleep at night, he said, as he watered some plants that grew in a couple of old car tires just before the trailer steps. He falls asleep, screams like somebody's killing him in his dreams, wakes up shaking like a leaf. How you going to cut your own child out of your heart and not scare yourself to death?

Did you ask Mom that question? I said.

He looked startled.

I just want to know, I said.

The day she mentioned her congregation advised her to stop letting you come home or talking to you on the phone, and she didn't say she'd told them to go to hell, I moved out.

I sat on the steps of the trailer in the blinding sun, thinking about the mystery of parents and their eternally unfathomable ways.

Well, I thought, *whatever*. I didn't send for my parents. My parents sent for me. But then I thought: What do I know. Maybe we sent for each other. Nobody knows how this stuff, Life, really works.

Hey, said my father, bringing me out of my reverie, you want some watermelon? He was lugging a huge dark green one out of the trailer. He'd grown it himself and was clearly proud.

Yes! I said, springing up.

It was the perfect thing.

As we ate this most beautiful of fruits, cool, thirst-relieving, delicious, I remembered there had been a time, *in my lifetime*, when black people were ashamed of watermelon, though they loved it with a passion. They would never want to be seen with or near a watermelon. They certainly never wanted to be seen eating one. If you'd photographed a black person eating watermelon in those days they probably would have considered killing you.

My father and I ate until we were stuffed, then we each claimed a sagging porch couch for a mid-afternoon nap.

We sure have come a long way, I said, drowsily, thinking of taking a sweet, juicy hunk of melon back to town for Mom, who, when I was growing up, would enjoy the deep pleasure of eating watermelon only in the privacy of her own kitchen, while leaning gluttonous and guilty over the kitchen sink.

But my father, his silver beard stained pink with watermelon juice, was already asleep.

The Way Forward Is With a Broken Heart

Epilogue

The Way Forward is with a Broken Heart

To the Husband of My Youth

It is the 16th of July, 1999. John Kennedy Jr.'s body has been found in waters off the coast of Martha's Vineyard. They say he 'hit a square' while flying his small aircraft; a situation in which it is impossible to tell up from down or earth from sky and that he lost his way. I've never heard this description before, and I don't immediately believe this is what happened to him; I am more inclined to think 'sabotage' or 'preemptive assassination,' but I like it immensely. Instantly I think of all the 'squares' I have hit. I think of you, from whom there is no word. No response to my call expressing concern for you after your mother's recent death.

Thinking of your mother, who never had the faintest notion what to make of me, non-Jewish, non-repentant, I know it is time to lay the past to rest. I say that, but am stunned to feel the absence, not of your mother, whom I rarely saw, but of a young man I never knew. Someone I never thought that much about. Saw only fleetingly on television or in the news, though his image was, apparently, everywhere, selling television, selling news. It's not that I wasn't aware of him; I just never pried into his life. The look I remembered came from thirty-five years ago when he was wearing snowsuits. The little face behind the smart military salute as his father's coffin rolled by. I look at his picture now and see someone who looks, above all, *decent*. A young man with good eyes and an open, honest face. Someone who barely noticed his own press.

I wonder how you are feeling about this? Did you gaze, as I did, at the faces of the three who died, trying to see if they had, before death, succeeded in finding the secret of life? To live it boldly, fully, without stinginess to the self? To find love and hold on to it until it walks away? To know that today is all we have, and maybe only a fraction of today? And that living life to the hilt is the best praise of it?

We have seen so many deaths! Our battered, trying to do our best with the mess we were left, generation. By now, not unlike the Kennedys, I imagine we are almost at the point of viewing the relentless approach of the Grim Reaper among those we love, coming ever closer to ourselves, as farce. We've wept so much. Up begins to rise in us something of the absurd.

I certainly feel this. I also feel, as someone I know has said, that these are the losses that mature us. They are also the losses that make us old. Did any of us expect to outlive the boy we called, as we assumed his family did, 'John-John'? Many of us never expected to outlive his father or his uncle or his cousins. It feels 'old' that we have. Remember how Bobby Kennedy came to Mississippi to find out for himself that black children were starving. And that he cried? And that he too, dying, was young?

We are no longer young, Stranger who was the husband of my youth. It is as elders that we are left behind by the young who are everywhere dying ahead of us, whether from starvation, war, assassination, or hitting 'squares,' of all forms. My heart aches for them.

We are not even the only ones not speaking to each other. Across America elders are not speaking to each other, though most of us will find we have a lot to say, after we've cried in each other's arms. We are a frightened, a broken-hearted nation; some of us wanting desperately to run back to the illusory 'safety' of skin color, money or the 1950s. We've never seen weather like the weather there is today. We've never seen violence like the violence we see today. We've never seen greed or evil like the greed and evil we see today. We've never seen tomatoes either, like the ones being created today. There is much from which to recoil.

And yet, Stranger who perhaps I am never to know, the past doesn't exist. It cannot be sanctuary. Skin color has always been a tricky solace, more so now that the ozone has changed. After Nature is destroyed, money will remain inedible. We have reached a place of deepest emptiness and sorrow. We look at the destruction around us and perceive our collective poverty. We see that everything that is truly needed by the world is too large for individuals to give. We find we have only ourselves. Our experience. Or dreams. Our simple art. Our memories of better ways. Our knowledge that the world cannot be healed in abstract. That healing begins where the wound was made.

Now it seems to me we might begin to understand something of the meaning of earnest speaking and fearless listening; something of the purpose of the most ancient form of beginning to remake the world: remembering what the world we once made together was like.

I send you my sorrow. And my art.

In the sure knowledge that our people, the American race, lovers who falter and sometimes fail, are good.